D0943849

WHILE THE WOMEN ARE SLEEPING

BY JAVIER MARÍAS
AVAILABLE FROM NEW DIRECTIONS

A Heart So White

All Souls

Bad Nature, *or* With Elvis in Mexico

Dark Back of Time

The Man of Feeling

Tomorrow in the Battle Think on Me

When I Was Mortal

Written Lives

Your Face Tomorrow
Volume One: Fever and Spear
Volume Two: Dance and Dream
Volume Three: Poison, Shadow and Farewell

Javier Marías

WHILE THE WOMEN ARE SLEEPING

Translated by Margaret Jull Costa

A NEW DIRECTIONS BOOK

First published in Spain in 1990 as *Mientras ellas duermen* by Alfaguara, Grupo Santillana de Ediciones, S.A.: *While the Women Are Sleeping* contains ten of the original Spanish edition's stories.

Published by arrangement with Mercedes Casanovas Agencia Literaria, Barcelona.

Grateful acknowledgment is made to the magazines and anthologies where some of these stories originally appeared: *The Dedalus Book of Spanish Fantasy, Leopard II: Turning the Page, Leopard IV: Bearing Witness, The New Yorker, The Reading Room, The Threepenny Review,* and *Zoetrope.* In addition, "While the Women Are Sleeping" was published as a limited edition from The Thornwillow Press with monotypes by Wendy Mark.

The translator would like to thank Javier Marías, Annella McDermott, Palmira Sullivan, and Ben Sherriff for all their help and advice.

Manufactured in the United States of America
New Directions Books are printed on acid-free paper.
First published clothbound in 2010
Design by Semadar Megged

Library of Congress Cataloging-in-Publication Data
Marias, Javier.
[Mientras ellas duermen. English]
While the women are sleeping / by Javier Marias ; translated by Margaret Jull Costa.
p. cm.
First published in Spain in 1990 as Mientras ellas duermen.
ISBN 978-0-8112-1663-0 (hardcover : alk. paper)
ISBN 978-0-8112-1914-3 (pbk. : alk. paper)
1. Marias, Javier—Translations into English. 2. Short stories, Spanish—Translations into English. I. Costa, Margaret Jull. II. Title.
PQ6663.A7218M5413 2010
863'.64—dc22 2010002110

10 9 8 7 6 5 4 3 2 1

New Directions Books are published for James Laughlin
by New Directions Publishing Corporation
80 Eighth Avenue, New York 10011

CONTENTS

AUTHOR'S NOTE

Of the ten stories that make up this collection, a few perhaps require some explanation.

"Lord Rendall's Song" was first published in my anthology *Cuentos únicos* (Ediciones Siruela, Madrid, 1989) in apocryphal form, that is, attributed to the English writer James Denham and purportedly translated by me. For that reason, I also include at the beginning of the story the biographical note that appeared there, since some of the facts in it contribute, tacitly, to the story itself, which would, otherwise, remain incomplete.

"The Life and Death of Marcelino Iturriaga" was published in *El Noticiero Universal* (Barcelona, April 19, 1968). It was, I believe, my first published piece. I was sixteen when it appeared, although I see from my typewritten original that it was written on December 21, 1965, that is, when I was just fourteen (be kind, please). Perhaps the most interesting thing about it, however, is that it bears some similarity to another story of mine, "When I Was Mortal," written in 1993 and included in the story collection of the same name.

As regards "A Kind of Nostalgia Perhaps," I was asked to contribute a story to a Mexican anthology, the royalties for which would go towards helping children in the state of Chiapas, who would provide the illustrations for the book. The deadline was so short that I decided to adapt an earlier story "No More Love," which appeared in the collection *When I Was Mortal.* The English characters have been replaced by Mexicans, and the ghost is no longer a nameless rustic youth.

—Javier Marías, 2010

WHILE THE WOMEN ARE SLEEPING

For Daniella Pittarello, in gratitude
for all her useful knowledge

For three weeks, I used to see them every day and now I don't know what will have become of them. I probably won't ever see them again, at least not her—one tends to assume that summer conversations and even confidences will lead nowhere. Not that anyone has anything against that, not even me, even though I do wonder about them or perhaps miss them slightly. Only very slightly, as one misses everything that disappears.

I nearly always saw them at the beach, where it's difficult

to get a good look at anyone. Particularly so in my case, because I'm nearsighted and would rather see everything through a haze than return to Madrid with a kind of white mask on my otherwise tan face, and I never wear my contact lenses when I go to the beach or the sea, where they might be lost forever. Nevertheless, from the very first moment, I was tempted to rummage around in the bag in which my wife, Luisa, keeps my glasses case—well, the temptation came from her really, because she, if I may put it like this, was constantly transmitting to me the more peculiar activities of the more peculiar bathers around us.

"Yes, I can see him, but only vaguely, I can't make out his actual features," I would say when she, in an unnecessarily low voice, given the noise level on the beach, would point out some character she found particularly amusing. I would keep screwing up my eyes, reluctant to get my glasses out only to have to return them once more to their hiding place once my curiosity was satisfied. Then one day, Luisa, who knows the strangest and most insignificant things and is always surprising me with scraps of useful knowledge, passed me her straw hat—closer to hand than my hidden glasses since it was on her head—and advised me to look through its mesh. And I discovered that by peering through this screen I could see almost as well as with my contact lenses, more clearly in fact, although my field of vision was greatly reduced. From that point on, I myself must have become one of the more peculiar or eccentric beachgoers, bearing in mind that I often had a woman's straw hat, complete with ribbons, clamped to my face with my right hand while I scanned the length and breadth of the beach near Fornells, where we were staying. Luisa, without a word of complaint or a flicker of annoyance, bought another hat that she didn't like as much, because hers, with which she had intended to shade her face—her fine-featured, open, and as yet unlined face—became mine, not for my head, but for my eyes, the hat through which I saw.

One day, we were enjoying ourselves following the exploits of a small Italian sailor, that is, an insubordinate one-year-old wearing nothing but a sailor's hat, who, as we kept reporting to each other, was going around destroying not only the fortifications built in the sand by his siblings and older cousins but doubtless some of his progenitors' long-term friendships, and doing so with the same aplomb with which he drank the salt water (he seemed to swallow gallons) to the complete unconcern of the families accompanying him. He frequently lost his sailor's hat and then was left completely naked, lying on the shore like a spurned cupid. On another day, we followed the despotic comments and idle comings and goings of a middle-aged Englishman—the island was heaving with Brits—who kept up a kind of running commentary on the temperature, the sand, the wind and the waves, speaking as emphatically and grandiloquently as if he were uttering deep, long-pondered maxims or aphorisms. He had the virtue, one that is becoming increasingly rare, of believing that *everything* is important, or, rather, that everything that comes from oneself has the virtue of knowing itself to be unique. His slothful nature was evident in how he sat—his legs always inelegantly splayed—and in the fact that he never took off the green T-shirt with which he protected his barrel chest from the sun, not even to go into the water. Needless to say, he never swam and when he did wade into the sea, never very far, he only did so in pursuit of one of his offspring so as to photograph him or her in action from a better angle or closer up. With his green stomach—but not, for example, his chest—wet from the waves, he would return to the shore muttering further unforgettable pronouncements, which the wind promptly scattered, and pressing his camera to his ear, as if it were a radio, concerned, apparently, that it might have got splashed, a primitive way, I suppose, of checking that it had come to no harm. Or perhaps, we thought, it was some kind of camera-radio.

Then one day, we saw them, I mean they came to our attention, well, to Luisa's first and then to mine, through my seeing hat. From then on, they became our favorites, and, each morning, without realizing it, we would look for them first before choosing our spot and would then choose somewhere close to theirs. On one occasion, we arrived at the beach before them, but, shortly afterwards, saw them roar up on a gigantic Harley-Davidson, with him at the handlebars wearing a black helmet (with the straps hanging loose) and her clinging on to him, her long hair streaming behind her. I think what drove us to seek out their company was that they offered us a rare sight, one from which it's always hard to look away: the spectacle of one human being adoring another. In accordance with the old and still valid rule, it was he, the man, who did the adoring, and she, the woman, who was the appropriately indifferent idol (or perhaps she was just bored and wished she had something to complain about). She was beautiful, indolent, passive and, by nature, languid. Throughout the three hours we spent at the beach (they stayed longer, perhaps taking their siesta there and, who knows, remaining until sunset), she barely moved and was, of course, concerned only with her own beautification and cleanliness. She dozed or was, at any rate, lying down, eyes closed, on her front, on her back, on one side, on the other, covered in sunscreen, her gleaming arms and legs always fully extended so that no part of her would remain untanned, no fold in her skin, even her armpits, even her groin (nor, it goes without saying, her buttocks), because her bikini bottom was minuscule and revealed that she was entirely free of hair, which made one think (well, made me think) that she must have had a Brazilian wax before she arrived. Now and then she would raise herself into a sitting position and then spend a long time with her knees drawn up while she painted or polished her nails or, with a small mirror in her hand, scrutinized her face or shoulders for blemishes or unwanted hair. It was odd to see her holding the mirror to the most unlikely parts of her body (it must have been a magnifying mirror), not just to her shoulders, I mean, but to her elbows, her calves, her hips, her breasts, the inside of her thighs, even her navel. I'm sure her navel could never have had any fluff in it, and perhaps what its mistress wanted was to suppress it altogether. As well as her tiny bikini, she wore bracelets and various rings, never fewer than eight of the latter, distributed among her fingers. I rarely saw her venture into the water. It would be easy to describe her as a conventional beauty, but that would be a poor definition—too broad or too vague. Rather her beauty was unreal, which is to say ideal. It's what children think of as beauty and which is almost always (unless the children are already deviants) an immaculate beauty, unmarked, in repose, docile, gestureless, with very white skin and large breasts, round—or at least not almond-shaped—eyes, and identical lips, that is, with upper and lower lip identical, as if they were both lower lips: the kind of beauty you get in cartoons or, if you prefer, in advertisements, and not in just any advertisements, but those you see in pharmacies, deliberately devoid of any hint of sensuality that might trouble other women or the elderly, who are the people most often in pharmacies. And yet neither was it a virginal beauty, and although I wouldn't say it was a milky pale beauty—or perhaps "creamy" is the word, it was the kind that would take time to turn brown (her skin was glossy, but not golden)—like Luisa's beauty; it was a smooth, voluptuous beauty, but one that didn't cry out to be touched (except perhaps when clothed), as if it might melt at the slightest contact, as if even a caress or a gentle kiss could become violence or rape.

Her male companion doubtless felt the same, at least during daylight hours. He was what you might call fat or even gross or obese, and he must have been more than thirty years older. Like many bald men, he believed he could make up for his lack of hair by wearing what little he had brushed forward, Roman-style (it never works) and by cultivating an abundant mustache, and that he could disguise his age, in that particular setting, by wearing a two-tone swimsuit, that is, with the right leg lime green and the left purple, at least, such was his chosen attire on that first day, because, like her, he rarely wore the same suit twice. The two colors (the style of trunks never varied, only the colors) invariably seemed to clash, although they were always highly original combinations: blue grey and apricot, peach and rose mallow, ultramarine and Nile green. The trunks were as small as his bulbous body allowed—it was inappropriate to talk about them having legs, really—and this meant that his movements were always slightly constrained by the ever-present threat of a rip. For the fact is he was in constant, agile movement, video camera in hand. Whereas his companion remained completely immobile or idle for hours on end, he never ceased circling her, tirelessly filming her: he would stand on tiptoe, bend double, lie on the ground, face up and face down, take pan shots, medium shots, closeups, tracking shots and panoramic shots, from above and from below, full face, from the side, from behind (from both sides); he filmed her inert face, her softly rounded shoulders, her voluminous breasts, her rather wide hips, her firm thighs, her far from tiny feet, her carefully painted toenails, her soles, her calves, her hairless pubis and armpits. He filmed the beads of sweat provoked by the sun, probably even her pores, although that smooth uniform skin seemed to have no pores, no folds or bumps, and not a single stretch mark marred her buttocks. The fat man filmed her every day for hours at a time, with few breaks, always the same scene: the stillness and tedium of the unreal beauty who accompanied him. He wasn't interested in the sand or the water, which changed color as the day wore on, or the trees or the rocks in the distance, or a kite flying or a boat far off, or in other women, the little Italian sailor, the despotic Englishman, or Luisa. He didn't ask the young woman to do anything—to play games, to make an effort or to pose—he seemed content with making a visual record, day after day, of that naked statuary figure, of that slow docile flesh, that inexpressive face and those closed or perhaps fastidious eyes, of a knee bending or a breast tilting or a forefinger slowly removing a speck from a cheek. For him, that monotonous vision was clearly a perennial source of wonder and novelty. Where Luisa or I or anyone else would see only repetition and weariness, he must, at every moment, have seen a remarkable spectacle, as multiform, varied and absorbing as a painting can be when the viewer forgets about the other paintings waiting for him and loses all notion of time, and loses, too, therefore, the habit of looking, which is replaced or supplanted—or perhaps excluded—by the capacity to *see*, which is what we almost never do because it's so at odds with the purely temporal. For it is then that one *sees* everything, the figures and the background, the light, the composition and the shadows, the three-dimensional and the flat, the pigment and the line, as well as each brushstroke. That is, one sees both what is depicted and the rough surface of the canvas, and it is only then that one can paint the picture again with one's eyes.

They spoke little and only occasionally, in short sentences that never became conversation or dialogue, any hint of which died a natural death, interrupted by the attention the woman was giving to her body, in which she was utterly absorbed, and by the indirect attention the man was giving to her body too, through his camera lens. In fact, I don't recall him ever stopping to look at her directly, with his own eyes, with nothing between his eyes and her. In that respect, he was like me, for I, in turn, viewed them either through the veil of my myopia or through my magnifying hat. Of the four of us, only Luisa could see everything without difficulty or mediation because I don't think the woman looked at or even saw anyone, and she herself mostly used her mirror to scrutinize and inspect, and she often donned a pair of extravagant space-age sunglasses.

"The sun's hot today, isn't it? You should put more sunscreen on, you don't want to burn," the fat man would say, in an occasional pause in his circular tours of his adored one's body; and when he didn't receive an immediate answer, he would say her name, the way mothers say their children's names: "Inés. Inés."

"Yes, it's definitely hotter than yesterday, but I've put on some S.P.F. ten, so I won't burn," replied the body, Inés, reluctantly and barely audibly while, with a pair of tweezers, she plucked out a tiny hair from her chin.

And there the conversation would end.

One day, Luisa—because we did have conversations—said:

"To be honest, I don't know whether I'd enjoy being filmed like poor Inés. It would make me nervous, although I suppose if someone was doing it all the time, like the fat man, I'd get used to it in the end. And then perhaps I'd take as much care of myself as she does, although she's probably only so vigilant because she's constantly being filmed or because she'll see herself later on screen or maybe she does it for posterity's sake." Luisa rummaged around in her bag, took out a small mirror and studied her eyes, which, in the sun, were the color of plums, with iridescent flecks in them. "Then again, what kind of posterity would want to waste its time watching those tedious videos. Do you think he films her during the rest of the day, too?"

"Probably," I said. "Why limit yourself to the beach? I doubt he needs an excuse to see her naked."

"I don't think he films her because she's naked, but all the time, perhaps even when she's sleeping. It's touching really, he obviously thinks only of her. But I don't know that I would like it. Poor Inés. Not that she seems to mind."

That night, when we got into our double bed at the hotel, both at once, each on our own side, I lay thinking about the things we had said and which I have just set down in writing, and, unable to sleep, I spent a long time watching Luisa sleeping, in the dark, with only the moon to light her. Poor Inés, she had said. Her breathing was very soft, but still audible in the silence of the room, the hotel and the island, and her body didn't move, apart from her eyelids, beneath which her eyes were doubtless moving about, as if they couldn't get used to not doing at night what they did during the day. Perhaps the fat man is awake too, I thought, filming the beautiful Inés's perfectly still eyelids, or maybe he'll lift the sheets off her and very carefully arrange her body in different positions so as to film her sleeping. With her nightgown pulled up perhaps or with her legs apart if she isn't wearing a nightgown or pajamas. Luisa didn't wear a nightgown or pajamas in summer, but she did wrap the sheet around her like a toga, clasping it to her with both hands, although one shoulder or the nape of her neck would sometimes come uncovered, and then, if I noticed, I would always cover her up. I sometimes had to struggle a little to make sure I had enough of the sheet on my side of the bed. But this only happened in summer.

I got up and went over to the balcony to kill time until sleep came, and from there, leaning on the balustrade, I looked up at the sky and then down, and that was when I thought I saw the fat man sitting alone by the swimming pool, in darkness now, the water reflecting only the stars. I didn't recognize him at first because he wasn't sporting the mustache I'd become used to seeing every day, as I had that very morning, and because our eyes have to accommodate themselves to seeing, fully clothed, someone we have been used to seeing undressed. His clothes were as ugly and ill-coordinated as his two-tone swimsuits. He was wearing a baggy shirt, which looked black from my balcony (from a distance) but was probably patterned, and a pair of light-colored slacks that appeared to be a very pale blue, possibly a reflection from the near-invisible water, so close it would have splashed him had there been any waves. On his feet he wore a pair of red moccasins, and his socks (imagine wearing socks on the island) seemed to be the same color as his trousers, but again that might have been the effect of the moon on the water. He was resting his head on one hand and the corresponding elbow on the arm of a floral-patterned sun lounger—there were two models available at the poolside, striped and floral. He didn't have his camera with him. I hadn't realized they were staying at our hotel, since we had only ever seen them at the nearby beach, to the north of Fornells, in the mornings. He was alone, as motionless as Inés, although now and then he changed that drowsy, laid-back pose of head and elbow and adopted another apparently contrary position, his face buried in his hands, his feet drawn in, as if he were exhausted or tense or possibly laughing to himself. At one point, he took off one shoe or accidentally lost it, but he didn't immediately reach out his foot to recover it, but stayed like that, his stockinged foot on the grass, which gave him a helpless look, at least from my fourth-floor viewpoint. Luisa was sleeping, and Inés would be sleeping too; she probably needed at least ten hours' sleep to maintain her immutable beauty. I got dressed in the dark, taking care not to make any noise, and checked that Luisa was well wrapped up in her sheet-*cum*-toga. Unaware that I wasn't in the bed, she had yet somehow sensed it in her sleep, for she was lying diagonally now, invading my space with her legs. I went down in the elevator, not having looked to see what time it was, past the night porter sleeping uncomfortably, head on the counter, like a future decapitee; I had left my watch upstairs, and everything lay in silence, apart from the slight noise made by my black moccasins (*I* wasn't wearing socks). I slid open the glass door that led to the swimming pool and closed it again, once I was outside on the grass. The fat man raised his head, glanced over at the door and immediately noticed my presence, although he couldn't make me out, I mean, couldn't identify me in the dim light. For that reason, because he had spotted me at once, I spoke to him as I walked toward him and as the reflections of the moon in the water began to reveal me and change my colors as I approached.

"You've shaved off your mustache," I said, running my index finger over the place where a mustache usually grows and not quite sure that I should make such a comment. By the time he could reply, I had reached his side and sat down on another sun lounger, next to him, a striped one. He had sat up, his hands on the arms of his sun lounger and was looking at me slightly nonplussed, but only slightly, and without a hint of suspicion, as if he wasn't in the least surprised to see me—or, indeed, anyone—there. I think that was the first time I had seen him face on—without a camera to his eye and without a hat to mine—or simply from close up, and my sight was already accustomed to the dim light after the brief time I'd spent gazing out from the balcony. He had an affable face, alert eyes, and his features weren't ugly, simply fat, and he struck me as one of those handsome bald men, like the actor Michel Piccoli or the pianist Richter. He looked younger without his mustache, or perhaps it was the red moccasins, one of which lay upturned on the grass. Yet he must have been at least fifty.

"Oh, it's you. I didn't recognize you at first with your clothes on, we usually only see each other in our beach wear." He had said exactly what I had thought earlier, when I was upstairs. We had spent nearly three weeks seeing each other every day, and it was impossible that his busy eyes would not at some point have lingered, despite everything, on me or on Luisa. "Can't you sleep?"

"No," I said. "The air-conditioning in the room doesn't always help. You're better off out here, I think. Do you mind if I join you for a while?"

"No, of course not. My name's Alberto Viana," and he shook my hand. "I'm from Barcelona."

"I'm from Madrid," I said and told him my name. Then there was a silence, and I wondered whether I should make some trivial remark about the island or about vacations or some other almost equally trivial remark about the activities we had observed on the beach. It was my curiosity about those activities that had led me to his side by the pool, well, that and my insomnia, although I could have continued to struggle with that upstairs or even woken Luisa, but I hadn't. I was speaking almost in a whisper. It was unlikely anyone could hear us, but the sight of Luisa, and of the night porter, sound asleep, had given me the feeling that if I raised my voice I would disturb their slumbers, and my hushed tones had immediately infected or influenced the way Viana spoke.

"I've noticed that you're very keen on video cameras," I said after that pause, that hesitation.

"Video cameras?" he said, slightly surprised or as if to gain time. "Ah, I see. No, not really, I'm not a collector. It isn't the camera itself that interests me, although I do use it a lot, it's my girlfriend, whom you've seen, I'm sure. I only film her, nothing else, I don't experiment with it at all. That's fairly obvious, I suppose. You've probably noticed." And he gave a short laugh, half-amused, half-embarrassed.

"Yes, of course, my wife and I have both noticed. I think

she feels slightly envious of the attention you lavish on your girlfriend. It's very unusual. I don't even have a regular camera. But then we've been married for some time."

"You don't own a camera? Don't you like being able to remember things?" Viana asked me this with genuine bemusement. As I had imagined, his shirt did have a pattern, a multicolored blend of palm trees and anchors and dolphins and ships' prows, but nevertheless the predominant color was the black I had seen from above; his trousers and socks still appeared to be pale blue, bluer than my white trousers, which, like his, were exposed now not just to the moonlight, but to the moon's faint reflection in the water.

"Yes, of course I do, but you can remember things in other ways, don't you think? We all have our own camera in our memory, except that we don't always remember what we want to remember or forget what we would prefer to forget."

"What nonsense," said Viana. He was a frank fellow, not at all the cautious type, and he could say things without offending the person he was talking to. He gave another short laugh. "How can you compare what you can remember with what you can *see*, with what you can see again, just as it happened? With what you can see again over and over, ad infinitum, and even hit the pause button, which you couldn't do when you saw whatever it was for real? What nonsense," he said again.

"Yes, you're right," I agreed. "But you're not telling me that you film your girlfriend all the time so that you can remember her later, by watching her on the screen. Or perhaps she's an actress. She wouldn't have time really, given that you appear to film her every day. And if you film her every day, there isn't time for what you've taped even to begin to resemble forgetting and for you to feel the need to recall her in that faithful manner by watching her again on video. Unless you're keeping it for when you're both old and want to relive your stay here in Minorca hour by hour."

"Oh, I don't keep all my footage, no, only a few brief fragments, maybe amounting to one tape every three or four months. But they're all filed away in Barcelona. And, no, she isn't an actress, she's still very young. What I do here (and at home too) is wait for a day before I erase the previous day's tape, if you see what I mean. In all this time, I've only used two tapes, always the same ones. I record one today and keep it, then record another one tomorrow and keep that, and then, the day after, I record over the first one, erasing it that way. And so on and so forth, if you see what I mean. Mind you, I shouldn't think I'll have time to record much tomorrow because we're going back to Barcelona, my vacation's over."

"Oh, I see. But then, once you're home, what will you do, make a montage of everything you've filmed?"

"No, you don't see. Artistic videos are one thing, made in order to be filed away. They get put to one side, one tape every four months or so. But the daily recordings are a separate matter. Those get erased every other day."

It may have been the lateness of the hour (I had left my watch upstairs), but I had the feeling that I still didn't entirely understand, especially the second part of his explanation. Also I wasn't that interested in the direction the conversation had taken, about artistic videos (that's what he'd said, I heard him) and erased tapes, the day-to-day ones. I considered saying goodnight and going back up to my room, but I still wasn't feeling sleepy and I thought that, if I did go back, I would probably end up waking Luisa just so she'd talk to me. That wouldn't be fair, and it seemed best to talk to someone who was already awake.

"But," I said, "why do you film her every day if you erase it afterwards?"

"I film her because she's going to die," said Viana. He had stretched out his stockinged foot and dipped his big toe into the water, moving it slowly back and forth, his leg stretched right out, for he could only just reach, just far enough to touch the surface. I fell silent for a few seconds, and then, as I watched him slowly stirring the water, I asked:

"Is she ill?"

Viana pursed his lips and ran his hand over his bald head, as if he still had hair and was smoothing it, a gesture from the past. He was thinking. I let him think, but he was taking an awfully long time. I let him think. Finally, he spoke again, not to answer my last question, but my previous one.

"I film her every day because she's going to die, and I want to have a record of her last day, of what might be her last day, so that I can really remember it, so that when she's dead, I can see it again in the future as often as I wish, along with the artistic videos. Because I *do* like to remember things."

"But is she ill?" I asked again.

"No, she's not ill," he said, this time without pausing to think. "At least not as far as I know. But she'll die one day. You know that, everyone knows that, everyone is going to die, you and me included, and I want to preserve her image. The last day in anyone's life is important."

"Of course," I said, looking at his foot. "You're just being cautious; she might have an accident, for example." And I thought (but only briefly) that if Luisa were to die in an accident, I wouldn't have many images to remember her by, hardly any pictures at all. There was the odd photo around the house—ordinary photos, of course, not artistic ones—but only a few. I certainly didn't have any movies of her. Without thinking, I glanced up at the balcony from which I had observed Viana. There were no lights on in any of the balconies or rooms. Nor, therefore, in the room belonging to Inés and Viana. I wasn't there on our balcony now, no one was.

Viana was again immersed in thought, although now he had removed his foot from the water and placed it again—with the tip of the sock wet and dark—on the grass. I began to think that perhaps he didn't like the direction the conversation had taken, and again I considered saying goodnight and going up to my room, yes, I suddenly wanted to go up and see again the image of Luisa asleep—not dead—wrapped in her sheet; one shoulder might have come uncovered. But once begun, conversations can't be abandoned just like that. They can't be left hanging, by taking advantage of a distraction or a silence, unless one of the two people involved is angry. Viana didn't seem angry, although his alert eyes did seem even more alert and more intense; it was hard to tell what color they were in the light cast by the moon on the water: I think they were brown. No, he didn't seem angry, just slightly self-absorbed. He was saying something, not in a whisper now, but as if muttering.

"I'm sorry, what did you say?" I asked.

"No, it's not that I think she'll have an accident," he replied, his voice suddenly too loud, as if he had miscalculated the shift in tone between talking to himself and talking to someone else.

"Lower your voice," I said, alarmed, although there was no reason to feel alarmed, it was unlikely anyone would hear us. I again glanced at the balconies, but they all still lay in darkness; no one had woken up.

Startled by my order, Viana immediately lowered his voice, but he wasn't startled enough not to continue what he had begun to say so loudly. "I said it's not that I think she might have an accident. But she'll definitely die before me, if you see what I mean."

I looked at Viana's face, but he wasn't looking at me, he was gazing up at the sky, at the moon, avoiding my eye. We were on an island.

"Why are you so sure of that if she isn't ill? You're much older than her. The normal thing would be for you to die before her."

Viana laughed again and, stretching his leg out still further, dipped his whole stockinged foot into the water this time and began to move it slowly, heavily around, more heavily than before because now his whole foot—that fat, obese foot—was submerged.

"Normal," he said, laughing. "Normal," he repeated. "Nothing is normal between her and me. Or rather, nothing is normal as regards my relationship with her, and never has been. I've known her since she was a child. Don't you see, I adore her."

"Yes, I see that. It's obvious that you adore her. I adore my wife, Luisa, as well," I added, in order to counter what he clearly considered to be the extraordinary nature of his adoration of Inés. "But we're more or less the same age, and so it's difficult to know which of us will die first."

"You adore her? Don't make me laugh. You don't even own a camera. You're not even much interested in remembering her exactly as she was—were you to lose her—in being able to see her again when it will no longer be possible for you to look at her."

This time, fat Viana's remark did bother me a little, I found it impertinent. I noticed this because there was something wounded and involuntary about my ensuing silence, and something fearful too, as if suddenly I no longer dared to ask him anything and as if, from that moment, I had no option but to listen to whatever he chose to tell me. It was as if that abrupt, indelicate remark had taken over the conversation entirely. And I realized that my fear came also from his use of the past tense. He had said "exactly as she was" when referring to Luisa, when he should have said "exactly as she is." I decided to leave him and go back up to our room. I wanted to see Luisa and to sleep by her side, to lie down and reclaim my space in the double bed that would doubtless be identical to the one shared by Inés and Viana, modern hotel rooms being all the same. I could simply bring the conversation to a close. I was feeling rather angry. However, the silence lasted only a few seconds because Viana continued talking, without this pause I have made, writing, and it was too late then not to continue listening to him.

"What you say is very true, but it hardly takes a genius to work that out. It's actually quite hard to know who will die first, it's tantamount to wanting to know the order of our dying. And to know that, you have to be a part of that order, if you know what I mean. Not to disrupt it, that would be impossible, but to be a part of it. Listen, when I said that I adore Inés, I meant it literally. I adore her. It's not just a turn of phrase, a meaningless, garden-variety expression that you and I can share, for example. What you call 'adore' has nothing whatever to do with what I mean by 'adore,' we share the word because there is no other, but not the thing described. I adore her and have adored her ever since I first met her, and I know that I'll continue to adore her for many years to come. That's why it can't last much longer, because that feeling has been the same inside me for too many years now, without variation or attenuation. There will be no variation on my part, it will become unbearable, it already is, and because, one day, it will all become unbearable to me, she will have to die before me, when I can no longer stand my adoration of her. One day, I'll have to kill her, don't you see?"

Having said that, Viana lifted his dripping foot out of the water and rested it carefully and distastefully on the grass, the sodden silk sock out of the water.

"You'll catch cold," I said. "You'd better take off your sock."

Viana did as I suggested and immediately removed the drenched sock, mechanically, indifferently. For a few seconds, he held it, still distastefully, between two fingers and then draped it over the back of his lounger, where it began to drip (the smell of wet cloth). Now he had one bare foot: the other was still covered by a pale blue sock and a rabidly red moccasin. The bare foot was wet and the covered foot very dry. I found it hard to look away from the former, but I think that fixing my gaze on something was a way of deceiving my ears, of pretending that what mattered were Viana's feet and not what he had said, that one day he would have to kill Inés. I preferred to think he hadn't said that.

"What are you saying?" I didn't want to continue the conversation, but I said precisely the words that obliged him to do so: "Are you crazy?"

"Crazy? What I'm going to tell you now is, in my view, totally logical," replied Viana and he again smoothed his nonexistent hair. "I've known Inés since she was a child, since she was seven years old. Now she's twenty-three. She's the daughter of a couple who were great friends of mine until five years ago, but who no longer are—it's perfectly normal, they're furious that their eighteen-year-old daughter went off to live with a friend of theirs whom they'd always liked and respected, and now they want nothing more to do with me, and not even, almost, with her. I often used to go to their house and I'd see Inés, and I adored her. She adored me, too, but in a different way, of course. She couldn't know at the time, but I knew at once, and I decided to prepare myself, to wait eleven years until she came of age, I didn't want to act in haste and ruin everything, and during the last few months of that period, I was the one who had to hold her back. It's what people call 'fixation,' and what I call 'adoration.' Not that it was easy, mind, even girls of twelve or thirteen have boys chasing after them, absurd boys who want to play at being adults from early on. They lack all self-control and can cause the girls great harm. I worked out that by the time she was eighteen, I would be nearly fifty, and so I took good care of myself, for her sake, I took enormous care of myself, although I couldn't do anything about my weight—your metabolism changes as you get older—nor about my baldness, there's still no satisfactory remedy for that, and as I'm sure you'll agree, a toupee is too undignified, so I had to rule that out. But I spent eleven years going to gyms and eating healthily and having check-ups every three months—because I have an absolute horror of operations; avoiding other women, avoiding diseases; and, of course, preparing myself mentally: listening to the same records she listened to, learning games, watching loads of TV, children's programs and years of ads, I know all the jingles by heart. As for reading matter, well, you can imagine, first I read comics, then adventure books, a few romantic novels, Spanish literature when she was studying that at school, as well as Catalan literature, Manelic and the wolf and all that, and I still read whatever she happens to be reading, American writers mainly, there are hundreds of them. I've played a lot of tennis and squash, done a bit of skiing and, on weekends, I've often had to travel to Madrid or San Sebastián just so that she could go to the races, and here we've been to all the fiestas in all the villages to see the horses and their riders. You may also have noticed my motorcycle. When I had to, I learned the names and heights of every basketball player, although now she's lost interest in the game. And you've seen how I dress, although, of course, in summer, anything goes." And Viana made an eloquent gesture with his right hand, as if taking in his whole outfit. "Do you see what I'm saying: all these years, I've led a parallel existence to my own (I'm a lawyer, by the way, specializing in divorce), first a childhood existence then an adolescent one—I was the king of video games—and since I couldn't go to the movies with her, I'd go on my own to see all those teenage films about thugs and extraterrestrials. I've led a parallel existence, but one that lacks all continuity, because it's incredibly hard to keep up to date, young people's fads change all the time. You can't imagine what it's like. You said that you and your wife are about the same age, so your field of reference will be the same or very similar. You'll have listened to the same songs at the same time, you'll have seen the same movies and read the same books, followed the same fashions, you'll remember the same events and have experienced them with the same intensity and in the same years. It's easy for you. Just imagine if it wasn't like that, imagine the long silences in your conversations. And the worst thing would be having to explain everything, every reference, every allusion, every joke about your own past or your own age, your own time. You might as well not bother. I've had a long wait and, what's more, I've had to reject my own past and create—as far as possible—another one that coincides with hers, with what will become her past."

Viana paused for a moment, very briefly, as if a fly had brushed past him. It was night, our eyes were accustomed now to the darkness and to the light from the water. We were on an island, I had no watch. Luisa was sleeping and Inés was sleeping too, each in their respective rooms and double beds, perhaps lying diagonally across the bed because neither Viana nor I was by their side. Maybe they missed us in their sleep. Or maybe not, maybe they felt relieved.

"But all that effort's over now, it no longer matters. What matters is my adoration, my immutable adoration. That's so identical to what it was sixteen years ago that I can't see it changing in the near future. And it would be disastrous if it did change. I've been devoted to her for too long now, devoted to her growing up, to her education, I couldn't live any other way. For her, though, it's different. She's fulfilled her childhood dream, her childhood fixation—five years ago, she was as happy or even happier than I was when she came to live with me, because my house had been entirely designed around her and there was nothing she wanted that she didn't have. But her character is still developing, she's still very dependent on novelty, she's drawn to the outside world, she's looking around to see what else there is, what awaits her beyond me, and she's a little tired, I think. Not just of me, but also of our strange, anomalous situation, she misses having a conventional life, misses the close relationship she had with her parents. Don't think I don't understand that, on the contrary, I foresaw it would happen, but the fact that I understand doesn't help one iota. We all have our own life to lead, and we only have the one life, and none of us is prepared not to live that life according to our own desires—apart from those who have no desires, they're the majority actually. People can say what they like, and speak of abnegation, sacrifice, generosity, acceptance and resignation, but it's all false: the norm is for people to think they desire whatever comes their way, whatever happens to them, what they achieve as they go along or what's given to them, and they have no original desires. But whether those desires are preconceived or not, we each care about our own life and, compared with that, the lives of others matter only insofar as they're interwoven with and form part of our own life, and insofar as disposing of those lives without consideration or scruple could end up affecting our own; there are, after all, laws, and punishment might follow. My adoration is excessive—that's what makes it adoration. The length of time I had to wait was excessive too. And now I continue to wait, but the nature of that waiting has been turned on its head. Before, I was waiting to gain something, now all I can expect is for all this to end. Before, I was waiting to be given a gift, now I expect only loss. Before, I was waiting for growth, now I expect decay. Not just mine, you understand, but hers too, and that's something I'm not prepared for. You're probably thinking that I'm making too many assumptions, that nothing is entirely foreseeable; as I said before, the order of our dying is equally unforeseeable. You're probably thinking that life is unforeseeable too, and that maybe Inés won't tire of me or leave me. You're thinking that I might be wrong to fear the passing of time, that perhaps she and I will grow old together, as you suggested earlier and as you're convinced that you and your wife will, because I heard what you said, your words weren't lost on me. But if that were the case, if all those years together did lie ahead of us, my adoration would still lead me to the same situation. Or do you imagine that I could allow my adoration to die? Do you think I could watch her age and deteriorate without resorting to the sole remedy that exists, namely, that she should die first? Do you imagine that, having known her as a seven-year-old (a seven-year-old), I could bear to see Inés in her forties, much less her fifties, with no trace of childhood left? Don't be absurd. It's like asking some particularly long-lived father to endure and celebrate the old age of his own children. Parents refuse to see their children transformed into old people, they hate them and jump over them and see only their grandchildren, if they have any. Time is always opposed to what it originated—to what is."

Viana buried his face in his hands, as I'd seen him do from above, from the balcony, but not from down here, by the pool. And I saw then that this gesture had nothing to do with suppressed laughter, but with a kind of panic that nevertheless failed to negate a certain serenity. Perhaps he had to make that gesture precisely in order to cling on to his serenity. I again glanced up at my balcony and at the other balconies, but all still lay in silence, dark and empty, as if beyond the balconies, beyond the windows and net curtains, inside the repeated and identical rooms, no one was sleeping, no Luisa, no Inés, no one. But I knew they were sleeping and that the world was sleeping, its weak wheel stopped. Viana and I were merely the product of its inertia for as long as we were speaking. He went on speaking, his face still covered:

"That's why time offers no solution," he said. "Rather than allow my adoration to die, I would rather kill her, you understand; and rather than allow her to leave me, rather than allow my adoration to continue, without its object, I would also rather kill her. That, from my point of view, is perfectly logical. That's why I know what I will have to do one day, possibly far off in the future, I'll delay it for as long as possible, but it's only a matter of time. Just in case, though, you see, I video her every day."

"Haven't you ever considered killing yourself?" I blurted out. I had been listening to him not because I wanted to, but because I had the feeling there was nothing else I could do and that the best way of not taking part in the conversation was to say nothing, to behave as if I were the mere repository of his confidences, without offering any objections or advice, without refuting or agreeing or being shocked. But it seemed to me harder and harder to bring this conversation to a close, the path it had taken was interminable, or so it seemed. My eyes felt itchy. I wished Luisa's sheets would slide off and wake her up, that she would notice my absence and, like me, go out onto the balcony. That she would see me down below, by the swimming pool, in the feeble glow cast by the moon on the water, and summon me upstairs, that she would say my name and rescue me from this conversation with Viana; all she had to do was call. What a drag, I thought, as I sat listening to him, I'll have to read the newspapers closely from now on and each time there's a headline about a woman who has died at the hands of a man I'll have to read the whole article until I find their names, now I'll always fear that Inés could be the dead woman and Viana the man who killed her. Although it might all be lies, here on this island, while the women are sleeping.

"Kill myself? That wouldn't be right," answered Viana, removing his hands from his face. He looked at me with an expression more of amusement than surprise, and the corners of his mouth almost lifted in a smile, or so it seemed to me in the darkness.

"It would be much less right—if I've understood you correctly—for you to kill her just so that you can continue to adore her on tape once she's dead."

"No, you don't understand: it would be right for me to kill her for the reasons I've explained, no one willingly gives up his way of life if he has a fairly good idea of how he wants to live it, and I do, which is unusual. And, how can I put it, murder is a very male practice, just as execution is, but not suicide, which is as common among women as it is among men. Earlier, I mentioned that she had a glimmering of what lies beyond me, but the fact is that beyond me there is nothing. As far as she's concerned, there is nothing; she may not realize that, but she should. And if I were to kill myself, then that wouldn't be the case—and really beyond me there must be nothing, don't you see?"

Viana's foot appeared to have dried off, but, hanging on the back of the lounger, the sock was still dripping rapidly onto the grass. I felt as if I could feel its dampness on my own shod feet, I could imagine what it would be like to put that wet sock on. I took off my left shoe so as to scratch the sole of that foot with my black moccasin, the one on my right foot.

"Why are you telling me all this? Aren't you afraid I'll report you? Or talk to Inés in the morning?"

Viana interlaced his fingers behind his neck and leaned

back on his lounger, and his bald head touched the wet sock. He reacted at once and sat up again, as one does when a fly brushes one's skin. He put on the red moccasin he had taken off some time before, when I was still standing on our balcony, and this somehow dissipated any air of helplessness he might have had, and it occurred to me suddenly that the conversation might end.

"You can't report intentions," he said. "We leave for Barcelona tomorrow, you and I will never see each other again, we leave early, there'll be no time to go to the beach. Tomorrow, you'll have forgotten all about this, you won't want to remember, you won't take it seriously or remember me or this moment, you won't try to find out anything. You won't ask about us at the hotel, to check that Inés and I left together, that we paid the bill, that nothing happened in the night, when you were the only person awake, talking to me. You won't even tell your wife what we talked about, why trouble her with it, because deep down you don't want to believe me, you'll manage, don't worry." Viana hesitated for a moment, then went on: "You may not think so, but if you were to warn Inés, you would simply accelerate the process, and I would have to kill her tomorrow, do you understand?" He hesitated again, paused, looked up at the sky, at the moon, and down at the water, then repeated that gesture of panic, covering his face, and continued speaking. "And who's to say that you'd be able to speak to her tomorrow, who's to say that I haven't already killed her, tonight, a while ago, before I came down here, who's to say that she isn't already dead and that's why I'm talking to you now, anyone can die at any moment, they taught us that at school, we've all known it ever since we were children, we all have our place in the order of dying, you yourself left your own wife sleeping, but how do you know she hasn't died while you've been down here talking to me, perhaps she's dying at this very moment, you wouldn't have time to reach her, not even if you ran. How do you know it's not Inés who has died at my hands, and that's why I shaved off my mustache, a while ago, before you came down, before I came down? Or Inés *and* your wife? How do you know that both of them haven't died, while they were sleeping?"

I didn't believe him. Inés's ideal beauty would be resting, her eight rings on the bedside table, her voluminous breasts safely under the sheets, her breathing regular, her identical lips half-open like a child's, her hairless pubis leaving a slight stain, that strange nocturnal secretion women make. Luisa was asleep, I had seen her, her fine-featured, open, and as yet unlined face, her restless eyes moving beneath her eyelids, as if they couldn't get used to not doing at night what they did during the day, unlike Inés's eyes, which would probably be quite still now, during the sleep she needed to maintain her immutable beauty. Both were sleeping, that's why they didn't wake up or come out onto the balcony, Luisa hadn't died in my absence, however long that had been—I'd forgotten my watch. Instinctively, I glanced up toward the rooms, toward my balcony, toward all the balconies, and on one of them, I saw a figure wrapped in a sheet toga and heard it call to me twice, saying my name, as mothers say their children's names. I stood up. On Inés's balcony, though, whichever it was, there was no one.

(1990)

GUALTA

Until I was thirty years old, I lived quietly and virtuously and in accordance, as it were, with my biography, and it had never occurred to me that forgotten characters from books read during adolescence might resurface in my life, or even in other people's lives. Of course, I had heard people speak of momentary identity crises provoked by a coincidence of names uncovered in youth (for example, my friend Rafa Zarza doubted his own existence when he was introduced to *another* Rafa Zarza). But I never expected to find myself transformed into a bloodless William Wilson, or a portrait of Dorian Gray minus the drama, or a Jekyll whose Hyde was merely another Jekyll.

His name was Xavier de Gualta—a Catalan, as his name indicates—and he worked in the Barcelona office of the same company I worked for. His (highly) responsible position was similar to mine in Madrid where we met at a supper intended for the dual purpose of business and fraternization, which is why we both arrived accompanied by our respective wives. Only our first names were interchangeable (my name is Javier Santín), but we coincided in absolutely everything else. I still remember the look of stupefaction on Gualta's face (which was doubtless also on mine), when the headwaiter who brought him to our table stood to one side, allowing him to see my face for the first time. Gualta and I were physically identical, like twins in the cinema, but it wasn't just that: we even made the same gestures at the same time and used the same words (we took the words out of each other's mouths, as the saying goes), and our hands would reach for the bottle of (Rhine) wine or the mineral water (still), or our forehead, or the sugar spoon, or the bread, or the fork beneath the fondue dish, in perfect unison, simultaneously. We narrowly missed colliding. It was as if our heads, which were identical outside, were also thinking the same thing at the same time. It was like dining opposite a mirror made flesh. Needless to say, we agreed about everything and, although I tried not to ask too many questions, such was my disgust, my sense of vertigo, our lives, both professional and personal, had run along parallel lines. This extraordinary similarity was, of course, noted and commented on by our wives and by us ("It's extraordinary," they said. "Yes, extraordinary," we said), yet, after our first initial amazement, the four of us, somewhat taken aback by this entirely anomalous situation and conscious that we had to think of the good of the company that had brought us together for that supper, ignored the remarkable fact and did our best to behave naturally. We tended to concentrate more on business than on fraternization. The only thing about us that was not the same were our wives (but they are not in fact part of us, just as we are not part of them). Mine, if I may be so vulgar, is a real stunner, whilst Gualta's wife, though distinguished-looking, was a complete nonentity, temporarily embellished and emboldened by the success of her go-getting spouse.

The worst thing, though, was not the resemblance itself (after all, other people have learned to live with it). Until then, I had never seen myself. I mean, a photo immobilizes us, and in the mirror we always see ourselves the other way round (for example, I always part my hair on the right, like Cary Grant, but in the mirror, I am someone who parts his hair on the left, like Clark Gable); and, since I am not famous and have never been interested in movie cameras, I had never seen myself on television or on video either. In Gualta, therefore, I saw myself for the first time, talking, moving, gesticulating, pausing, laughing, in profile, wiping my mouth with my napkin, and scratching my nose. It was my first real experience of myself as object, something which is normally enjoyed only by the famous or by those who play around with video cameras.

And I hated myself. That is, I hated Gualta, who was identical to me. That smooth Catalan not only struck me as entirely lacking in charm (although my wife—who is gorgeous—said to me later at home, I imagine merely to flatter me, that she had found him attractive), he seemed affected, prissy, overbearing in his views, mannered in his gestures, full of his own charisma (commercial charisma, I mean), openly right-wing in his views (we both, of course, voted for the same party), pretentious in his choice of words and unscrupulous in matters of business. We were even official supporters of the most conservative soccer clubs in our respective cities: he of Español and I of Atlético. I saw myself in Gualta and in Gualta I saw an utterly repellent individual, capable of anything, potential firing squad material. As I say, I unhesitatingly hated myself.

And it was from that night, without even informing my wife of my intentions, that I began to change. Not only had I discovered that in the city of Barcelona there existed a being identical to myself whom I detested, I was afraid too that, in each and every sphere of life, at each and every moment of the day, that being would think, do and say everything exactly the same as me. I knew that we kept the same office hours, that he lived alone, without children, with his wife, exactly like me. There was nothing to stop him living my life. I thought: "Everything I do, every step I take, every hand I shake, every word I say, every letter I dictate, every thought I have, every kiss I give my wife, will be being done, taken, shaken, said, dictated, thought, given to *his* wife by Gualta. This can't go on."

After that unfortunate encounter, I knew that we would meet again four months later, at the big party being given to celebrate the fifth anniversary of our company, American in origin, and now being set up in Spain. And during that time, I applied myself to the task of modifying my appearance: I cultivated a mustache, which took a long while to grow; sometimes, instead of a tie, I would wear an elegant cravat; I started smoking (English cigarettes); and I even tried to disguise my receding hairline with a discreet Japanese hair implant (the kind of self-conscious, effeminate thing that neither Gualta nor my former self would ever have allowed himself to do). As for my behavior, I spoke more robustly, I avoided expressions such as "horizontal integration" or "deal dynamics" once so dear to Gualta and to myself; I stopped pouring wine for ladies during supper; I stopped helping them on with their coats; I would even occasionally swear.

Four months later, at that Barcelona celebration, I met a Gualta who was sporting a stunted mustache and who appeared to have more hair than I remembered; he was chain-smoking John Players and instead of a tie, he was wearing a bow tie; he kept slapping his thighs when he laughed, digging people with his elbow, and exclaiming frequently: "fucking hell!" I found him just as hateful as before. That night, I too was wearing a bow tie.

From then on the process of change in my own abominable person really took off. I conscientiously sought out everything that an excessively suave, smooth, serious, sententious man like Gualta (he was also very devout) could never have brought himself to do, and at times and in places when it was most unlikely that Gualta, in Barcelona, would be devoting his time and space to committing the same excesses as me. I began arriving late at work and leaving early, making coarse remarks to the secretaries, I would fly into a rage at the slightest thing and frequently insult my staff and I would even make mistakes, never very serious ones, but which a man like Gualta, however—so punctilious, such a perfectionist—would never have made. And that was just at work. As for my wife, whom I always treated with extreme respect and veneration (until I turned thirty), I managed, gradually, subtly, to persuade her not only to have sex at odd times and in unsuitable places ("I bet Gualta is never this daring," I thought one night as we lay together, in some haste, on the roof of a newspaper kiosk in Calle Príncipe de Vergara), but also to engage in sexual deviations that only months before, in the unlikely event of our ever actually having heard of them (through someone else, of course), we would have described as humiliating or even as sexual atrocities. We committed unnatural acts, that beautiful woman and I.

After three months, I awaited with impatience my next encounter with Gualta, confident that now he would be very different from me. However, the occasion did not arise and, finally, one weekend, I decided to go to Barcelona myself with the intention of watching his house in order to discover, albeit from afar, any possible changes in his person or in his personality. Or, rather, to confirm the efficacy of the alterations I had made to myself.

For eighteen hours (spread over Saturday and Sunday) I took refuge in a café from which I could watch Gualta's building and wait for him to come out. He did not appear, however, and, just when I was wondering whether I should return defeated to Madrid or go up to his apartment, even if I risked possibly bumping into him, I suddenly saw his nonentity of a wife come out of the front door. She was rather carelessly dressed, as if her spouse's success were no longer sufficient to embellish her artificially or as if its effect did not extend to weekends. On the other hand, though, it seemed to me, as she walked past the darkened glass concealing me, that she was somehow more provocative than the woman I had seen at the supper in Madrid and at the party in Barcelona. The reason was very simple and it was enough to make me realize that I had not been as original as I thought nor had the measures I'd taken been wise: the look on her face was that of a salacious, sexually dissolute woman. Though very different, she had the same slight (and very attractive) squint, the same troubling, clouded gaze as my own stunner of a wife.

I returned to Madrid convinced that the reason Gualta had not left his apartment all weekend was because that same weekend he had travelled to Madrid and had spent hours sitting in La Orotava, the café opposite our building, waiting for me to leave, which I had not done because I was in Barcelona watching his house which he had not left because he was in Madrid watching mine. There was no escape.

I made a few further, but by now rather half-hearted, attempts. Minor details to complete the transformation: like becoming an official supporter of Real Madrid, in the belief that no supporter of Español would ever be allowed into Barça; or else I would order anisette or aniseed liqueur—drinks I find repugnant—in some dingy bar on the outskirts, sure that a man of Gualta's refined tastes would not be prepared to make such sacrifices; I also started insulting the Pope in public, certain that my rival, a fervent Catholic, would never go that far. In fact, I wasn't sure of anything and I think that now I never will be. A year and a half after I first met Gualta, my fast-track career in the company for which I still work has come to an abrupt halt, and I expect to be fired (with severance pay, of course) any day now. A little while ago, without any explanation, my wife left me, either because she had grown weary of perversion or else, on the contrary, because my fantasies no longer sufficed and she needed to go in search of fresh dissipations. Will Gualta's nonentity of a wife have done the same? Is his position in the company as precarious as mine? I will never know, because I prefer not to now. For the moment has arrived when, if I did arrange to meet Gualta, two things could happen, both equally terrifying, or at least, more terrifying than uncertainty: I could find a man utterly different from the one I first met and identical to the current me (scruffy, demoralized, shiftless, boorish, a blasphemer and a pervert) whom I will, however, possibly find just as awful as the Xavier de Gualta I met the first time. As regards the other possibility, that's even worse: I might find the Gualta I first met, unchanged: impassive, courteous, boastful, elegant, devout and successful. And if that were the case, I would have to ask myself, with a bitterness I could not bear, why, of the two of us, had I been the one to abandon and renounce my own biography?

(1986)

ONE NIGHT OF LOVE

My sex life with my wife, Marta, is most unsatisfactory. My wife is neither very lascivious nor very imaginative, she never whispers sweet nothings and usually yawns whenever I happen to be in the mood. That's why I occasionally go to prostitutes, but even they have grown increasingly nervous as well as increasingly expensive, and monotonous too, not to mention unenthusiastic. I would much prefer it if my wife, Marta, were more lascivious and imaginative and that I could be satisfied with her alone. I was happy on the one night when she did satisfy me.

Among the things my father left me when he died is a

packet of letters that still gives off a faint whiff of cologne. I don't believe the sender actually perfumed the letter herself, but rather, I assume that, at some point in his life, my father kept the letters near a bottle of cologne that one day spilled onto them. You can still see the stain, and so the smell is clearly that of the cologne my father both used and didn't use (given that the contents were spilled), and not that of the woman who sent him the letters. Moreover, the smell is characteristic of him, a smell I knew very well, that never changed and which I've never forgotten, the same throughout my childhood and adolescence and a good part of my youth, an age in which I am still installed or have not yet abandoned. That is why, before age diminished my interest in things amorous or passionate, I decided to read the letters he bequeathed to me and about which, up until then, I had felt no curiosity at all.

The letters were written by a woman who was and still is called Mercedes. She wrote in black ink on blue paper. Her handwriting is large and maternal, made with rapid strokes of the pen, as if she no longer aspired to making an impression, doubtless aware that she had already caused an impression that would last forever. It's as if the letters had been written by someone who had already died when she wrote them, like letters from beyond the grave. I can't help th`inking that it was some kind of game, one of those games of which children and lovers are so fond, and that consist basically in pretending to be what you're not, or, put another way, in giving each other fictitious names and creating fictitious lives, afraid perhaps (this applies to lovers, not children) that their overpowering feelings will destroy them if they admit that they, with their real lives and names, are the people having those feelings. It's a way of blunting the most passionate and most intense of emotions, pretending that the whole thing is happening to someone else; it's also the best way of observing it, of being an aware spectator. Yes, experiencing it and, at the same time, being aware of it.

The woman who signed herself Mercedes had opted for the fiction of sending her love to my father after she had already died, and so convinced was she of the eternal place and time she occupied while writing them (or so sure that the addressee would accept this convention) that she appeared entirely unconcerned by the fact that she had to entrust her envelopes to the post-box or that they bore the normal stamps and postmarks of the city of Gijón. They were all dated, and the only thing missing was a return address, but that is more or less obligatory in any semi-clandestine affair (the letters all belong to the period of my father's widowhood, but he never spoke to me of this late passion). Nor is there anything unusual about the existence of this correspondence—though I have no idea whether my father replied in the usual way—for there is nothing more commonplace than widowers in sexual thrall to bold, fiery (or disillusioned) women. The declarations, promises, demands, reminiscences, outbursts, protests, exclamations and obscenities (especially obscenities) that fill these letters are conventional enough and remarkable less for their style than for their audacity. None of this would be of any interest if, only a few days after deciding to open the packet and peruse the blue sheets with rather more equanimity than shock, I myself had not received a letter from that woman called Mercedes, of whom I couldn't say: She's still alive, because she seems to have been dead from the start.

Her letter was very proper, and she didn't presume a relationship with me simply because she had once been on intimate terms with my father, nor was she so vulgar as to translate her love for the father, now that he was dead, into an unhealthy love for his son, who was and is still alive and was and is still me. Seemingly completely unembarrassed that I should know about their relationship, she restricted herself to setting before me an anxiety, a complaint and a demand for the presence of her lover, who, despite his repeated promises, had still not joined her six months after his death: he had failed to meet her in the place or perhaps I should say time agreed. This, in her view, could be put down to one of two reasons: to a sudden, last-minute cooling of his affections at the moment of death that would have caused the deceased to break his promise, or to his having been buried and not cremated (as he had requested), and which—according to Mercedes, who spoke of this as if it were the most natural thing in the world—could prevent or obstruct their eschatological meeting or reunion.

It was true that despite my father's request to be cremated, although he had not insisted on it (perhaps because he made this request only at the end, when his will power was weakened), he had nevertheless been buried alongside my mother, because there was space for him in the family vault, and Marta and I felt it was the appropriate, sensible, convenient thing to do. Mercedes' letter seemed to me a joke in the very worst taste. I threw it in the trash can and was even tempted to do the same with the old letters too. Like them, the new envelope bore fresh stamps and was postmarked in Gijón. It didn't smell of anything though. I wasn't prepared to disinter my father's remains merely in order to set fire to them.

The next letter arrived soon afterwards, and in it, Mercedes, as if she could read my thoughts, begged me to cremate my father because she could not go on living (that's what she said, go on living) in that state of uncertainty. Rather than continue waiting for him for all eternity, possibly in vain, she would prefer to know that my father had decided not to rejoin her. In this letter, she still addressed me with the formal *usted*. I can't deny that I was fleetingly moved (that is, *while* I was reading the letter, not afterwards), but the conspicuous Asturias postmark was too prosaic for me to be able to see it as anything but a macabre joke. The second letter took its place in the trash can as well. My wife, Marta, saw me tearing it up and asked:

"What is it that's annoyed you so much?"

My gestures must have been somewhat violent.

"Oh, nothing," I said and carefully gathered up the pieces so that she wouldn't be able to put them back together again.

I waited for a third letter, which, precisely because I did wait for it, took longer than expected to arrive or perhaps time spent waiting just seems longer. It was quite different from the previous letters and resembled those my father used to receive. Mercedes addressed me now with the familiar *tú*, and offered me her body, if not her soul. "You can do what you like with me," she said, "whatever you can imagine or wouldn't even dare to imagine doing to someone else. If you grant my plea to disinter and cremate your father and allow him to rejoin me, you will never forget me for as long as you live, not even when you die, because I will gobble you up, and you will gobble me up." I believe I blushed when I read this for the first time, and for a fraction of a second I toyed with the idea of going straight to Gijón to offer myself to her (I'm drawn to the weird and the dirty in sex). But then I immediately thought: "How absurd. I don't even know her last name." That third letter, however, did not end up in the trash can. I still have it hidden away.

It was about then that Marta underwent a change of attitude. I don't mean that, from one day to the next, she stopped yawning and became a woman of unbridled passion, but she did begin to show a greater interest in and curiosity about me and my no longer very young body, as if she sensed an infidelity on my part and was on the alert, or as if she herself had been unfaithful and wanted to find out if some newly discovered technique might be possible with me as well.

"Come here," she would say sometimes, and she had never made such overtures to me before. Or she would utter a few words, for example: "Yes, yes, now."

The third letter that had promised so much had left me waiting for a fourth letter even more anxiously than the second irritating letter had left me waiting for the third. But no fourth letter arrived, and I realized that I was beginning to wait for the mail each day with growing impatience. I noticed that my heart turned over whenever an envelope arrived bearing no return address, and then my eyes would glance rapidly at the postmark, to see if it was from Gijón. But no one ever writes from Gijón.

Months passed, and on All Souls' Day, Marta and I took flowers to my parents' grave, in which my grandparents and my sister are also buried.

"What will happen to *us*, do you think?" I said to Marta, as we breathed in the clean cemetery air from a bench close to our family vault. I was smoking a cigarette, and she was studying her nails, holding her spread fingers some distance from her, like someone urging a crowd to remain calm. "I mean, when *we* die. There's no room here now."

"The things you think about."

I gazed off into the distance in order to give myself an appropriately dreamy air that would justify what I was about to say, and I said:

"I'd like to be buried. Burial is more suggestive of repose than cremation. My father wanted to be cremated, do you remember, and we didn't do what he wanted. We should have, I think. It would bother me to think that my wish to be buried were ignored. What do you think? I'm thinking we ought to disinter him. That way, there'd be room for me when I die. You could go to your parents' vault."

"Let's get out of here. You're beginning to give me the creeps."

We set off among the graves, towards the exit. It was sunny. But we had only gone a few steps, when I stopped, looked at the tip of my cigarette and said:

"Don't you think we should cremate him?"

"Do what you like, but let's get out of here."

I threw down my cigarette and buried it in the ground with my foot.

Marta refused to attend the ceremony, an emotionless affair of which I was the sole witness. My father's remains went from being vaguely recognizable in his coffin to being entirely unrecognizable in an urn. It didn't seem to me necessary to scatter the ashes and, besides, that's not allowed.

When I got home, late, I felt quite depressed; I sat down in my armchair without taking off my coat or turning on the light and stayed there, waiting, musing, thinking, perhaps recovering from the responsibility and the effort of having done something I should have done some time ago, of having fulfilled a wish (someone else's wish), while, in the background,

I could hear distant sounds of Marta taking a shower. After a while, my wife, Marta, emerged from the bathroom wearing her pink robe and with her hair still wet. She was lit from behind by the light from the still steamy bathroom. She sat down on the floor at my feet and rested her damp head on my lap. After a few seconds, I said:

"Shouldn't you dry yourself off? You're making my coat and trousers wet."

"I'm going to make all of you wet," she said and revealed that she was naked beneath her bathrobe. We were both now lit by the distant light from the bathroom.

That night, I was happy because my wife, Marta, was both lascivious and imaginative, whispering sweet nothings to me, and she didn't yawn once, in short, I was satisfied with her alone. I'll never forget that. It hasn't happened since. It was a night of love. No, it hasn't happened again.

A few days later, I received the long-awaited fourth letter. I still haven't dared to open it, and sometimes I feel tempted simply to tear it up and never read it. This is partly because I think I know and fear what the letter will say; unlike the previous three addressed to me, it smells slightly of cologne, a cologne I have not forgotten and that I know well. I haven't experienced another night of love, which is why, precisely because it hasn't happened again, I sometimes have the odd sense that, on that one night, I betrayed my father or that my wife, Marta, betrayed me with him (perhaps because we gave each other fictitious names and created lives that were not our own), although the truth is that on that night, in our apartment, in the dark, lying on her bathrobe, only Marta and I were there. Just Marta and me.

I haven't experienced another night of love nor have I ever

again felt that she alone could satisfy me, and so I still go to prostitutes, who are increasingly expensive and increasingly nervous. Perhaps I should try transvestites. Not that I really care, it doesn't worry me and won't last, although it might for a while. Sometimes I find myself thinking that, when the time comes, it would be easiest and most convenient if Marta were to die first, because that way I could bury her in the place in the vault that was left vacant. That way, I wouldn't have to explain why I've changed my mind, because now I would prefer to be cremated; in fact, under no circumstances do I want to be buried. On the other hand—I surprise myself thinking—I don't know that I would gain much from that because my father will have taken his place, my place, next to Mercedes, for all eternity. When I'm cremated—I surprise myself thinking—I'll have to bump off my father, although I don't know how you can bump off someone who's already dead. Sometimes I wonder if the letter I haven't yet opened says something quite different from what I imagine and fear, whether it offers me a solution, whether she perhaps expresses a preference for me. Then I think: "How absurd. We've never even met." I look at the letter, sniff it, turning it over in my hands, and always end up hiding it away again, still unopened.

(1989)

LORD RENDALL'S SONG

For Julia Altares who has not yet discovered me

James Ryan Denham (1911–1943), born in London and educated at Cambridge, was one of the ill-starred talents of the Second World War. The son of a well-to-do family, he embarked on a diplomatic career that took him to Burma and India (1934–1937). His known literary work is scant and hard to come by, consisting of five now unobtainable books, all published in private editions, since it would seem he never considered this activity to be anything more than a hobby. He was a friend of both Malcolm Lowry, whom he had met in college, and of the famous art collector Edward James, and he himself came to own a fine collection of eighteenth- and nineteenth-century French paintings.

His last book, How to Kill *(1943), from which this story, "Lord Rendall's Song," is taken, was the only one he tried to publish in a commercial edition; however, at the time, with the country still at war, he was unable to find a publisher willing to accept it, partly because of the depressing effect it was felt the book might have on civilians and soldiers alike and partly because of the oddly erotic undertone present in some of the stories. Before that, Denham had published a book of poetry,* Vanishings *(1932), another volume of short stories,* Knives and Landscapes *(1934), a short novel,* The Night-Face *(1938), and* Gentle Men and Women *(1939), a series of sketches of famous people, among them Chaplin, Cocteau, the dancer Tilly Losch and the pianist Dinu Lipatti. Denham died when he was thirty-two-years old, killed in action in North Africa.*

Although the story published here (a vertiginous mise en abîme*) is self-explanatory, it might be useful to know that the popular English song "Lord Rendall" consists of a dialogue between the young Lord Rendall and his mother after the former has been poisoned by his lover. To his mother's final question, "What will you leave your sweetheart, Lord Rendall, my son?" he replies: "A rope to hang her, mother, a rope to hang her."*

I wanted to give Janet a surprise and so I decided not to tell her exactly when I would be home. Four years, I thought, is such a long time that a few more days of uncertainty will not make any difference. Getting a letter on Monday informing her that I would be arriving in two days would be far less exciting than finding me there on our doorstep when she opened the front door on Wednesday itself. I had left war and imprisonment far behind me now, and so quickly had they been left behind that I was already beginning to forget them. I would gladly have forgotten it all instantly so that I could do my best to ensure that my life with Janet and our son would be unaffected by my sufferings, so that I could pick up my life again just as if I had never gone away, as if my time at the front—along with the orders and the fighting and the lice, the mutilations, hunger and death—had never existed. Nor the terror and the torments of the German prisoner-of-war camp. She knew I was alive, she had been notified to that effect, she knew that I had been taken prisoner and was therefore alive and would come home. She must have been waiting daily for some word of my return. I'd give her a surprise, not a fright, and that would be a good thing. I would knock at the door and she would open it, drying her hands on her apron, and there I would be, dressed in civilian clothes at last, looking rather ill and thin, but nonetheless smiling and longing to embrace and to kiss her. I would take her in my arms, untie her apron, and she would bury her face in my shoulder and weep. I'd notice my jacket growing damp with her tears, so very different from the constant dripping of the damp punishment cell or the monotonous rain falling on our helmets during marches and in the trenches.

From the moment I made that decision not to announce my arrival, I enjoyed the anticipation of my return so much that when I finally found myself standing outside the house, I almost regretted having to put an end to that sweet waiting. And that was why I first crept round to the back, hoping I might hear or see something from the outside. I wanted to accustom myself to all the usual, familiar sounds again, the sounds I had missed so dreadfully all the time I had been kept from them: the kitchen clatter of pots and pans, the creaking bathroom door, Janet's footsteps. And the child's voice. The child had been one month old when I left, and then he only used his voice to scream and shout. He would be four now and would have a real voice, and his own way of talking, perhaps like his mother's, since he would have spent all that time alone with her. His name was Martin.

I could not be sure if they were at home or not. I got as far as the back door and held my breath, eager for sounds. The first thing I heard was a child crying and I found that odd. It was the crying of a small child, as small as Martin had been when I left for the front. How was that possible? I wondered if I had got the wrong house or if Janet and the child had moved away without my knowing and another family had moved in. The baby's crying came from far off, apparently from our bedroom. I peered in. There was the kitchen, empty, no one there, no food. Night was falling, it was about time Janet started preparing something for supper; perhaps she would do so as soon as the child had calmed down. I could not wait, however, and I walked round to the front of the house to see if I had any better luck there. On my right was the living room window, on my left, on the other side of the front door, our bedroom window. I walked round the house to the right, keeping close to the wall, half crouching so as not to be seen. Then I slowly drew myself up until I could see into the living room with my left eye. That was empty too, the window was closed but I could still hear the child crying, the child who could not possibly be Martin. Janet must be in the bedroom, calming the child down, whoever that child was, and always assuming that the woman was Janet. I was just about to move over to the window on the left when the living room door opened and I saw Janet come in. It was her, I hadn't got the wrong house and no, they hadn't moved away without my knowing. She was wearing an apron, just as I had pictured her. She always wore an apron; she said taking it off was a waste of time because she would only have to put it on again later to do something else. She looked very pretty, she hadn't changed. I saw and thought all this in a matter of seconds, because behind her, immediately behind, I saw a man following her in. He was very tall and from my perspective his head was cut off by the upper frame of the window. He was in shirtsleeves, but still had his tie on, as if he had just come home from work and so far had only had time to take off his jacket. He seemed very much at home. When he came in, he had walked behind Janet the way husbands in their own homes walk behind their wives. If I crouched any lower, I would be unable to see anything, so I decided that I would wait until he sat down to get a good look at his face. He turned round for a few seconds, presenting me with a close-up view of the back of his white shirt, his hands in his trouser pockets. When he moved away from the window, I could see Janet again. They did not speak. They seemed angry. It was one of those brief, tense silences that tend to follow marital arguments. Then Janet sat down on the sofa and crossed her legs. I thought it odd that she should be wearing sheer stockings and high heels when she had her apron on. She suddenly buried her face in her hands and started crying. He crouched down by her side, but not to console her; he was just watching her cry. And it was then that I saw his face. His face was *my* face. The man in shirtsleeves looked exactly like me. I do not mean that he bore an unusually close resemblance to me: his features were identical to mine, they were mine; it was like looking at myself in a mirror or, rather, like watching one of those home movies we made shortly after Martin was born. Janet's father had given us a movie camera so that we could see our child when he was no longer a child. Janet's father had had money before the war and I hoped that, despite any financial difficulties, Janet would have been able to film something of the years with Martin that I had lost. I even wondered if what I was seeing was, in fact, a film. Perhaps I had arrived at precisely the moment when Janet, feeling nostalgic, had chosen to sit down in the living room to watch one of those movies showing scenes that took place before I went away. No, that was impossible, for what I was watching was in color, not black and white and, besides, no one had ever filmed us from that window—what I was seeing I was seeing from the position I was occupying at that moment. The man in the room was real: if I broke the glass and reached in, I could touch him. He was crouching by the sofa and he had my eyes, my nose, my lips, my blond curly hair, he even had the small scar at the base of his left eyebrow from the time my cousin Derek threw a stone at me when I was a child. I touched the small scar. Outside, night had fallen.

He was talking now, but I couldn't make out what he was saying through the closed window and Martin had stopped crying since they went into the living room. Meanwhile, Janet was still sobbing and the man who looked like me was crouched beside her, saying something to her, though I could tell from the expression on his face that his words were not consoling but mocking or even accusing. My head was in a whirl, but despite that, two or three ideas still surfaced in my mind, each more absurd than the last. I thought she must have found a man identical to me in order to take my place during my long absence. I thought that time must have been incomprehensibly altered or cancelled, that those four years actually had been forgotten, erased, just as I had wished, and that I really might be able to pick up the threads of my life with Janet and the child again. The years of war and imprisonment really hadn't existed and I, Tom Booth, had never gone to war or been taken prisoner which was why I was here, as on any other day, arguing with Janet on my return from work. I had spent those four years with her. I, Tom Booth, had not been called up, I had stayed at home. But then, who was the "I" looking through the window, the "I" who had walked up to this house, the "I" who had just been released from a German P.O.W. camp? Who did all these memories belong to? Who had fought in the war? And I thought something else too, maybe the excitement of returning home had evoked some scene from the past, a scene, maybe the very last scene, that took place before I went away, something I had forgotten and that resurfaced now with the shock of homecoming. Perhaps, on that last day, Janet had cried because I was going away, possibly to my death, and I had treated it all as a joke. That might explain the child Martin's crying, for he was still a baby then. The fact was, however, that it was no hallucination, I was neither imagining nor remembering it, I was seeing it now. Besides, Janet had not cried before I left. She was a woman of great strength of character, she had kept smiling right up until the very last moment, she had behaved as if it were the most natural thing in the world, as if I were not really going away at all. She knew that any other attitude would have made everything so much more difficult for me. She would weep today when I opened the door, but this time she would weep on my shoulder, making my jacket damp with her tears.

No, I wasn't seeing something from the past, something I had forgotten. I knew this with absolute certainty when I saw the man, the husband, the man who was me, Tom, suddenly stand up and seize Janet by the throat, his wife, my wife, sitting there on the sofa. He seized her round the throat with both hands and I knew that he had begun to squeeze even though, again, all I could see was Tom's back, my back, the vast white shirt blocking my view of Janet who was still sitting on the sofa. Of her I could see only her outstretched arms, her arms flailing in the air and then hidden behind the shirt, in desperate attempts to loosen the grip which was not my grip; and then, after a few short seconds, Janet's arms appeared again, fallen on either side of the shirt of which I could see only the back, except this time they were limp, inert. Through the closed windows I could hear the child crying again. The man left the room, going off towards the left, doubtless towards the bedroom where the child was. And when he moved away, I saw Janet there dead, strangled. In the struggle her skirt had ridden up and she had lost one of her high-heeled shoes. I saw the garters I had tried so hard not to think about during those last four years.

I was paralyzed, but I managed to think: that man who is me, that man who has not moved from Chesham during all this time, is going to kill Martin as well or else the new baby, assuming that Janet and I have had another baby during my absence. I must break the glass and go in and kill that man before he kills Martin or his own newborn child. I must stop him. I must kill myself right now. Except that I am outside the window and the danger is inside.

While I was thinking all this, the child's crying stopped, suddenly. There were none of the little whimpers you usually get as a child calms down, none of the progressive calm that overtakes children when you pick them up or rock them or sing to them. Before I went away, I used to sing Lord Rendall's song to Martin and sometimes I managed to soothe him, to stop him crying, but it took a long time, I had to sing the song over and over. He would go on sobbing, but his sobs would gradually diminish, until at last he fell asleep. That child, on the other hand, had fallen silent abruptly, with no transitional phase. And in that new silence, without realizing what I was doing, I stood up and started singing Lord Rendall's song by the window, the song I used to sing to Martin and which begins: "Where have you been all the day, Rendall, my son?" except I used to sing: "Where have you been all the day, Martin, my son?" And then, when I began singing it there next to the window, I heard the voice of the man in our bedroom join me to sing the second verse: "Where have you been all the day, my pretty Tom?" But the child, my child Martin or his child who bore my name, had stopped crying. And when the man and I stopped singing Lord Rendall's song, I could not help wondering which of the two of us would be hanged.

(1989)

AN EPIGRAM OF FEALTY

For Montse Mateu

Mr. James Lawson looked up. He had just that morning rearranged the window display of the bookstore of which he was manager, Bertram Rota Ltd, Long Acre, Covent Garden, one of the most prestigious and discriminating second-hand bookstores in London. He preferred not to overcrowd the window, displaying, at the most, ten carefully chosen books or manuscripts, each one of which was extremely valuable. They were the sort of editions guaranteed to attract his usual clientele which consisted exclusively of distinguished gentlemen and the occasional elegant lady bibliophile. That morning, with some pride, he had placed in the window works such as *Salmagundi* by William Faulkner, never reprinted after that first 1932 edition (of 525 numbered copies), and the first edition of *Jacob's Room* by Virginia Woolf, priced at £2,000. Although he himself set the prices according to the state of the market, he could still never get used to the fact that a book could be worth so much money. But those books were nothing compared with Beckett's novel, *Watt*, typed and corrected by the author himself and priced at £50,000. He had had his doubts about putting such a valuable item in the window, but in the end, he had decided to go ahead. It was a source of great satisfaction to him and, after all, he would be there all morning and all afternoon, stationed at his desk, keeping guard over the window. Nonetheless, he felt uneasy and looked up from his desk whenever he noticed someone, some figure, standing on the other side of the glass. He even looked up when people walked past. This time, however, he kept his head raised, for before him, at the window, was a wild-looking beggar. His hair was rather long and he sported a few days' growth of reddish beard. He was well-built and had a large, apparently broken nose. His clothes, like those of any mendicant, were shabby and of some indefinable color. In his right hand he held a half-empty bottle of beer. He wasn't drinking, though, he did not from time to time raise the bottle to his lips, rather he was utterly absorbed, staring into the window of Bertram Rota. Mr. Lawson wondered what he could be looking at. At Camus? One of the books on display was a copy of *La Chute* dedicated by the author himself and open at the appropriate page. But *La Chute* was on the right-hand side, next to the typescript of *Watt* and the beggar was looking to the left. On that side Lawson had placed *Salmagundi* and the second 1839 edition of *Oliver Twist*, priced at £300. Dickens was possibly of more interest to the beggar than Faulkner. He might have read Dickens at school, but not Faulkner, for the man was at least sixty years old, and possibly older.

Mr. Lawson looked down for a moment, believing (though without really thinking it) that perhaps this would make the beggar disappear. He immediately looked up again and found, to his surprise, that the man had indeed gone, there was no one there. He got up and, standing slightly on tiptoe, checked that everything in the window was still in order. Perhaps he should remove Watt, all £50,000 of it, or perhaps display only the first few pages, He returned to his seat and for a couple of minutes gave all his attention to the new catalogue he was compiling, but again he noticed a change in the light (someone was blocking the light coming from the street) and he felt obliged to look up. The beggar was back, bottle in hand (the beer would be completely flat by now), this time accompanied by two other beggars, each more ragged than the other. One was a young black man wearing green mittens and a large earring in one ear; the other, the same age as the first man, had a domed head that made the jockey's cap with which he tried to cover it seem even smaller; the cap (purple and white, although the purple had faded and the white was now yellow) was covered with large, greasy stains. The beggar with the reddish beard was urging them to draw nearer and when he had persuaded them to do so, all three of them stared in through the window, again at the left-hand side of the display, and the first beggar kept pointing at something with one grimy finger. He did so with pride, for afterwards, he would turn to his companions, first to the black man and then to the jockey, with obvious satisfaction.

Was it Salmagundi or Dickens they were looking at? There was another item there too, a curious document consisting of an eight-page pamphlet which, in the previous catalogue, Lawson had entitled An Epigram of Fealty. It contained three poems by Dylan Thomas never published elsewhere. Lawson opened a drawer and took out the catalogue in which it had first appeared, the 250th since the founding of Rota, and rapidly re-read the description: "Printed privately for the members of the Court of the Kingdom of Redonda [1953]." Seventeen years ago. "Thirty commemorative copies, each numbered by John Gawsworth himself. Very rare. These three poems, not listed in Rolph's bibliography of Thomas, are testaments to the poet's 'fealty' to John Gawsworth, Juan I, King of Redonda, who, in 1947, named Thomas 'Duke of Gweno.' £500." Five hundred pounds, not bad for a few printed pages, thought Lawson. Perhaps that was what the beggars were looking at. He noticed that the one with the beard was now pointing at himself, tapping his chest with his forefinger. The others were also pointing, but in the way one points one's finger at someone else, at a person deserving of ridicule. Now the three of them were talking and arguing. Though Lawson could hear nothing of what they said, he was beginning to feel worried. Why had they chosen to stand for so long outside his store window of all places? Not that sales at Rota depended on passing trade, but their disquieting presence would certainly scare off any potential distinguished customers (only distinguished people bought books at Rota). He couldn't get rid of them though, they weren't breaking any law, they were simply looking at a window full of old books. But that particular window contained the typescript of Watt, and Watt was worth £50,000.

Lawson stood up and went over to them, still keeping to his side of the glass. Perhaps they would go away if they saw him watching them from inside. He folded his arms and fixed them with his blue eyes. He knew that one glance from those cold, blue, unfriendly eyes had often proved an effective deterrent in the past, one which he intended to deploy now to intimidate those three beggars. But the beggars were still embroiled in their argument, taking not the slightest notice of him, or else his presence, closer now, remained a matter of complete indifference to them. Now and then, the first beggar would again point at the window and Lawson was certain now that the focus of his interest was the *Epigram*. Lawson could stand it no longer. He opened the door and addressed them from the threshold:

"Can I be of any assistance?"

The beggar with the reddish beard looked Lawson up and down, as if he were an intruder. He was considerably taller than Lawson, indeed, despite his years and his wretched appearance, he was very solidly built. The man could easily have knocked him to the ground, thought Lawson, or else the other two could have held him down whilst the first beggar grabbed and made off with the *Epigram* or, worse still, with the typescript of *Watt* worth £50,000. He regretted having opened the door. He was exposing himself to attack.

"Yes, yes, you can," said the beggar after a pause of a few seconds. "Tell my two friends here who the King of Redonda was. You must know."

Lawson looked at him, perplexed. Hardly anyone knew anything about the King of Redonda, only a handful of bibliophiles and scholars, people of great learning, experts. He saw no reason, however, not to reply.

"His name was John Gawsworth, although in fact his real name was Armstrong. Quite by chance, he inherited the title of King of Redonda or Redundo, an uninhabited island in the Antilles, of which he never actually took possession. He did, however, set about creating an aristocracy, bestowing a few fictitious titles on friends, like this one given to the poet Dylan Thomas," explained Lawson, indicating the pamphlet to his left. "He was only a very minor writer. Why are you interested in him?"

"You see, isn't that what I told you? How else could I possibly know all that?" said the tall beggar, turning to the other two. Then to Lawson he said: "How much are you selling the *Epigram* for?"

"I'm not sure you could afford it," said Lawson in paternalistic tones, feigning hesitancy. "It's worth £500."

The jockey with the domed cranium jibed: "Yeah, £500 that won't be coming your way. Why don't you give us a few of your other books and we can sell them all to this gentleman?"

"Shut up, you idiot, I'm telling you the truth. That pamphlet was mine once and the loyalty expressed in it was dedicated to me." And turning to Lawson again, the man with the beard added: "Do you know what became of John Gawsworth?"

Lawson was growing weary of the conversation.

"I don't actually. I think he died. He's an obscure figure." And Lawson looked at the typescript of *Watt*, fortunately still there (no one inside the store, none of the other employees, had stolen it while he, like a fool, was standing at the door with these three beggars).

"No, sir, there you're wrong," said the beggar. "You're right about him being a minor writer and an obscure figure, but he isn't dead. Though these two fellows here won't believe me, I am John Gawsworth. I am the King of Rcdonda.

"Oh, come now," said Lawson impatiently. "Stop cluttering up the pavement and move away from this window. You're drunk, the lot of you, and if you stumbled against the glass, you could break it and injure yourselves. Be off with you." And with a rapid movement he slipped back into the store and bolted the door.

He returned to his desk and sat down. The beggar was looking at him coldly now from the other side of the glass. He seemed offended. He was angry. His brown eyes were genuinely cool, unfriendly, intimidating, more so than Lawson's own cool, blue, intimidating eyes. The other two beggars were laughing and jostling the tall beggar as if to say: "Come on, let's go" (though Lawson could hear nothing) . The first beggar, however, remained quite still, as if rooted to the pavement, staring at Lawson coldly, threateningly. Lawson could not hold his gaze. He looked down and tried to immerse himself once more in the compilation of the next catalogue, the 251st since the founding of Rota, the discriminating bookstore of which he was manager. That way perhaps he'll disappear again, he thought. If I don't look at him, don't see him, he'll disappear, the way he did before. Although, of course, then he came back.

He kept his eyes lowered until he noticed a change in the light. Only then did he dare to look up to see that the window was clear. He got to his feet and went over to check the display again. On the pavement lay a shattered beer bottle. But there, safe and sound, awaiting their distinguished bibliophile purchasers, were *Salmagundi*, £350, *Oliver Twist*, £300, *La Chute*, £600, *Jacob's Room*, £2,000, *An Epigram of Fealty*,

£500, and *Watt*, £50,000. He gave a sigh of relief, picked up the typescript of *Watt* and clasped it to him. It had been typed by Beckett himself, who had never trusted anyone else with the task. Perhaps he should withdraw it from display, it was after all worth £50,000. He carried it back to his desk to consider the matter and there, for a moment, allowed himself an absurd thought. A copy of *An Epigram of Fealty* bearing John Gawsworth's signature would be worth twice as much. A thousand pounds, he thought. Lawson looked up, but the window was still empty.

(1989)

A KIND OF NOSTALGIA PERHAPS

It is quite possible that the main aim of ghosts, if they still exist, is to thwart the desires of mortal tenants, appearing if their presence is unwelcome and hiding away if it is expected or demanded. There have, however, been instances of pacts made between ghosts and mortals, as we know from various documents collected by Lord Halifax and Lord Rymer in England and by Don Alejandro de la Cruz in Mexico.

One of the most modest and touching of these cases is that of an old lady living in Veracruz, around 1920, when she was not an old lady, but a young girl who knew nothing of such visitations and waitings—or are they perhaps a kind of nostalgia? In her youth, this old lady had been the companion of a wealthy widow of advancing years, to whom, among other services rendered, she used to read in order to ease the tedium of her mistress's lack of visible needs and preoccupations, and of a premature widowhood for which there was no remedy: for, according to people in that port city, Señora Suárez Alday had suffered the occasional illicit disappointment in love after her brief marriage, and it was probably this—rather than the death of her slightly or entirely unmemorable husband—that had made her seem curt and withdrawn at an age when such characteristics in a woman are no longer considered intriguing or charming or a fit topic for teasing. Boredom made her so lazy that she was barely able to read by herself, in silence and alone, so she had her companion read out loud to her details of affairs and feelings which, with each day that passed—and they passed very quickly and monotonously—seemed more and more alien to that house. The lady always listened very intently, utterly absorbed, and only occasionally asked her companion (Elena Vera by name) to repeat a passage or a piece of dialogue to which she did not wish to bid farewell forever without, first, making some attempt to hold on to it. When Elena finished reading, her only remark was: "Elena, you have a lovely voice. You will find love with that voice."

And it was during these sessions that the ghost of the house first made his appearance. Every evening, while Elena was speaking the words of Cervantes or Dumas or Conan Doyle, or verses by Darío or Martí, she could just make out the figure of a young man of somewhat rustic appearance, a man of about thirty or so, who politely removed his broad-brimmed hat and whose perfectly decent clothes were, nevertheless, full of holes, as if he, or, rather, the short jacket, white shirt and tight trousers that clothed his absent body, had been riddled with bullets. The latter, however, seemed quite unscathed, and his face, barricaded behind a bushy mustache, had a healthy glow. The first time she saw him standing there—leaning his elbows on the back of the chair occupied by her mistress, occasionally playing with the hat he held in his hand, as if listening, rapt, to the words she was reading—she almost cried out with fright, especially when she saw that, although he wasn't carrying any weapons, he did have a cartridge belt slung across his chest. But the young man immediately raised one finger to his lips and made reassuring signs to Elena, indicating that she should continue and not betray his presence. He had a very inoffensive face, and there was in his mocking eyes a constant, shy smile that occasionally gave way, during certain somber passages—or perhaps when he was assailed by thoughts or memories of his own—to the alarmed, naive seriousness of someone who cannot quite distinguish between what is real and what is imagined. And so the young woman obeyed, although that first day, she could not help but keep glancing up rather too frequently and staring at a point above the bun on her mistress's head, so much so that Señora Suárez Alday also kept glancing anxiously up, as if wondering whether some hypothetical hat were awry or whether her halo were not quite bright enough. "Whatever's wrong, child?" she said, somewhat annoyed. "What do you keep looking at?" "Nothing," said Elena Vera, "it's just a way of resting my eyes before going back to the text. Reading for such a long time is tiring." The young man with the scarf about his neck nodded and raised his hat for a moment in a gesture of approval and gratitude, and her explanation meant that the young woman could thereafter continue the habit and thus at least satisfy her visual curiosity. For, from then on, evening after evening and with very few exceptions, she read for her mistress and for him, without the former ever once turning round or discovering the young man's intrusive presence.

He did not appear at any other moment, so Elena never had the opportunity, over the years, of speaking to him or asking who he was or had been or why he was listening to her. She considered the possibility that he might have been the cause of the disappointment in love suffered by her mistress at some time in the past, but her lady never offered any confidences, despite the promptings of all those sentimental or tragic pages read out loud and despite the hints dropped by Elena herself during the slow, nocturnal conversations of half a lifetime. Perhaps the local rumors were false and the lady had no adventures worth telling, which was why she enjoyed hearing about the most remote and foreign and improbable of tales. On more than one occasion, Elena was tempted to take pity on her and tell her what was going on each evening behind her back, to allow her to share this small daily excitement, to tell her of the existence of a man between those ever more asexual, taciturn walls in which there was only the echo, sometimes for whole nights and days together, of their female voices, the lady's grown ever older and more confused, and Elena's, each morning, a little weaker and fainter, a little less lovely, a voice that, contrary to her mistress's predictions, had not brought her love, not at least of the permanent, tangible kind. But whenever she was about to give in to that temptation, she would suddenly remember the young man's discreet, authoritative gesture—one finger on his lips, repeated now and then with a slightly teasing look in his eyes—and so she kept silent. The last thing she wanted was to make him angry. Perhaps ghosts got as bored as widows did.

One day, Elena noticed a sudden change in the expression on the face of that man, half-peasant, half-soldier, with the holes in his clothes which she always felt an impulse to sew up, so that the night chill from the sea air would not slip through them. Señora Suárez Alday's health began to decline, and a few days before her death (although no one knew then that she would die so soon) she asked Elena to read from the Gospels rather than from novels or poems. Elena did as she requested and noticed that whenever she pronounced the name "Jesús"—which was often—the man would grimace in pain or sorrow, as if the very name hurt him. By the tenth or eleventh time, the pain must have become unbearable, because his always rather diffuse, but nonetheless perfectly distinguishable body grew gradually more and more tenuous until it disappeared altogether, long before she had concluded her reading session. Elena wondered if the man had been an atheist, an enemy of official religions. To clarify this, she insisted, a couple of days later, on reading her mistress a novel much praised by the critics, *Enriquillo*, by the Dominican author Manuel de Jesús Galván. And before beginning her reading, she spoke a little to her mistress about the novelist, making a point of saying his whole name and never just his surname; and she saw that whenever she pronounced the name "Jesús," her visitor shrank back and his eyes shone with a mixture of fury and fear. Elena came to suspect something that had, for a long time, seemed unimaginable, and as she read the book, she invented a very brief dialogue, in which she had Enriquillo address an inferior in these terms: "Hey, you, Jesús, *guajiro*." The ghost covered his eyes in terror for a moment, utterly shaken. Elena did not insist and the man regained his composure.

Elena kept back her final test for another three days. Her mistress was growing weaker, but she nonetheless refused to stay in bed and sat in her armchair as if that sign of health would be a safeguard against death. And Elena expressed an interest in *The Travels of Marco Polo*, or so she said, because, in fact, what really interested her was the prologue and the biographical note about the traveler. She introduced a few words of her own, saying: "This great adventurer traveled to China and to Mecca, among other places." She stopped, and feigning surprise, added: "Imagine that, Señora, what a long journey, all the way to China and to Mecca." The man's tan weather-beaten face turned deathly pale and, at the same time and without transition, how can we put it, his entire figure abruptly vanished, as if that ashen pallor had erased him from the air, made him transparent, a nothing, invisible even to her. And then she was sure that the man was Emiliano Zapata, murdered in his thirties by the treachery of a supposed *zapatista* called Jesús Guajardo, in a place called Chinameca, or so the legend goes. And she felt very honored to think that she was being visited by the ghost of Zapata, his clothes still full of the holes made by those treacherous bullets.

Her mistress died the next morning. Elena stayed on in the house, and for a few days, saddened and disoriented, with no reason to continue, she stopped reading. The young man did not appear. And then, convinced that Zapata wanted to have the education he had doubtless lacked in life, and persuaded by the idea that in his lifetime he had suffered from an excess of reality and for that reason, after death, wished to find repose in fictions, but also fearful that this was not the case and that his presence had somehow been mysteriously linked to the old lady—a love affair with Zapata required more secrecy than any other, a secret that would have to be kept forever—she decided to go back to reading out loud in order to call him back, and she read not only novels and poetry, but books on history and the natural sciences. The young man took some time to reappear—perhaps ghosts go into mourning, for who else has more reason to or perhaps they are still wary, perhaps words can still wound them—but he did finally return, attracted perhaps by the new material, and he continued to listen with the same close attention, not standing up this time, leaning on the chairback, but comfortably installed in the now vacant armchair, his hat dangling from his hand, and sometimes with his legs crossed and holding a lit cigar, like the patriarch he never, in his numbered days, had had the chance to become.

The young woman, who was growing older, jealously guarded her secret and spoke ever more confidingly to him, but never received a reply: ghosts cannot always speak nor do they always want to. And as that one-sided intimacy grew, so the years passed, and she was always careful not to mention the name "Jesús" again in any context and to avoid any words that resembled "*guajiro*" or "Guajardo" and to exclude forever from her readings any references to China or Mecca. Then one day, the man failed to appear, nor did he in the days and weeks that followed. The young woman, who was now almost old herself, was worried at first like a mother, fearing that some grave accident or misfortune might have befallen him, not realizing that such things only happen to mortals, that those who are no longer mortal are quite safe. When she understood this, her worry turned to despair: evening after evening, she would stare at the empty armchair and curse the silence, she would ask sorrowful questions of the void, hurl reproaches into the invisible air, and curse the past to which she feared he had returned; she wondered what mistake or error she could have made and searched eagerly for new texts that might arouse the *guerrillero*'s curiosity and make him come back—new topics and new novels, new adventures of Sherlock Holmes, for she put more faith in Conan Doyle's narrative skills than in any other scientific or literary bait. She continued to read out loud every day, to see if he would come.

One evening, after months of desolation, she found that the bookmark she had left in the Dickens novel she was patiently reading to him in his absence was not where she had left it, but many pages ahead. She carefully read the pages he had marked, and then, bitterly, she understood, experiencing the disappointment that comes in every life, however quiet and recondite. There was a sentence in the text that said: "And she grew old and lined, and her cracked voice was no longer pleasing to him." Don Alejandro de la Cruz says that the old lady became as indignant as a rejected wife, and that, far from accepting this judgement and falling silent, she reproached the void thus: "You are most unfair, but in life, so they say, you always tried to be scrupulously fair. You do not grow old, and want to listen to pleasant youthful voices, and to contemplate firm luminous faces. I can understand that; you're young and always will be, and you may not have had much time, and many things escaped you. But I have educated and amused you for years; and if, thanks to me, you have learned much, possibly even how to read, it hardly seems right that you should leave me offensive messages in the very books I have shared with you. Bear in mind that when the old lady died, I could easily have read in silence, but I didn't. I could have left Veracruz, but I didn't. I know that you can go in search of other voices, nothing binds you to me and it's true that you've never asked me for anything—you owe me nothing. But if you have any notion of gratitude, Emiliano," and this was the first time she called him by his name, still not knowing if anyone was listening, "I ask you to come at least once a week and to have patience with my voice, which is no longer a beautiful voice and no longer pleases you, and now will never bring me love. I will try hard to read as well as I can. But do come, because now that I'm old, I need you to amuse and keep me company. I would miss seeing you and your bullet-riddled clothes. Poor Emiliano," she added more calmly, "all those bullets."

According to the scholarly Don Alejandro de la Cruz, the ghost of that rustic man and eternal soldier, who may have been Zapata, was not entirely lacking in sympathy. He accepted her reasoning or felt that he owed her a debt of gratitude: and from then until her death, Elena Vera awaited with excitement and impatience the arrival of the day chosen by her impalpable, silent love to return—from the past, from a time in which, in fact, neither past nor time existed—the arrival of each Wednesday, when he was perhaps coming back from Chinameca, murdered, sad, exhausted. And it is thought that those visits, that that listener and their pact, all kept her alive for many more years, in that city facing the sea, because with him she still had a past and a present and a future too—or perhaps they too are a kind of nostalgia.

(1998)

THE RESIGNATION LETTER OF SEÑOR DE SANTIESTEBAN

For Juan Benet, fifteen years late

Whether it was one of those bizarre occurrences to which Chance never quite manages to accustom us, however often they may arise; or whether Destiny, in a show of caution and prudence, temporarily suspended judgment on the qualities and attributes of the new teacher and so felt itself obliged to delay intervening just in case such an intervention should later have been found to be a mistake; or whether, finally, it was because in these southern lands even the boldest and most confident of people tend to distrust their own gifts of persuasion, the fact of the matter is that young Mr. Lilburn did not discover what truth there might be in the strange warnings issued to him—only a few days after he had joined the Institute—by his immediate superior, Mr. Bayo, and by other colleagues too, until he was well into the first term when sufficient time had elapsed for him to be able to forget or at least to postpone thinking about the possible significance of the warnings. Mr. Lilburn, in any case, belonged to that class of person who, sooner or later, in the course of a hitherto untroubled life, finds his career in ruins and his unshakable beliefs overturned, refuted and even held up to ridicule by just such an event as concerns us here. And so it would, therefore, have made little difference if he had never been asked to stay behind to lock up the building.

Lilburn, who was just thirty-one, had eagerly accepted the post offered him, through Mr. Bayo, by the director of the British Institute in Madrid. Indeed, he had experienced a certain sense of relief and something very like the discreet, imperfect, muted joy felt in such situations by men who—while they wouldn't ever dare to so much as dream of rising to heights they had already accepted would never be theirs—nevertheless expect a small improvement in their position as the most natural thing in the world. And although his work at the Institute did not, in itself, constitute any improvement at all, either economic or social, with respect to his previous position, young Mr. Lilburn was very conscious, as he signed the rather unorthodox contract presented to him by Mr. Bayo during the latter's summer sojourn in London, that, while spending nine months abroad was almost an invitation to people in his native city to forget all about him and his abilities, and implied, too, the loss—perhaps not, he imagined, irrevocable—of his comfortable but extremely mediocre post at the North London Polytechnic, it also brought the distinct possibility of coming into contact with people higher up the administrative ladder and, more importantly, with prestigious members of the diplomatic corps. Furthermore, having dealings, for example (why not?), with an ambassador could prove most useful to him—however sporadic and superficial those dealings might be—possibly in the not too distant future. And so, around the middle of September, and with the indifference characteristic of any only moderately ambitious man, he made his preparations, recommending a far less knowledgable replacement for the post he was vacating at the Polytechnic, and arrived in Madrid, determined to work hard if necessary to earn the esteem and trust of his superiors—with an eye to any future advantages this might bring him—and to resist being seduced by the flexibility of the Spanish working day.

Young Lilburn soon managed to establish an orderly life for himself in that foreign land and, after a few initial days of vacillation and relative bewilderment (the days he was obliged to spend in the house of old Mr. Bayo and his wife while he waited for the previous tenants to vacate the small furnished attic apartment in Calle de Orellana reserved for him from October 1st by Mr. Turol, another of his Spanish colleagues; the rent was too high for Lilburn's budget, but it wasn't really expensive if one took into account that it was extremely central and had the incomparable advantage of being very near the Institute), he set himself a meticulous and—if such a thing were possible throughout a whole academic year—invariable daily routine, and which he did, in fact, manage to maintain, although only until the month of March. He got up at seven on the dot and, after breakfasting at home and briefly going over what he planned to say in each of his morning classes, set off to the Institute to teach. During break-time, he would share with Mr. Bayo and Miss Ferris his dismay at the Spanish students' appalling lack of discipline and then, over lunch, would make the same remarks to Mr. Turol and Mr. White. Over dessert, he would review the afternoon's lessons, which he would take at a rather slower pace than he had in the morning, and, once they were over, would spend from six to half past seven in the Institute's library, consulting a few books and preparing his classes for the next day. He would then walk to the elegant house of the widowed Señora Giménez-Klein, in Calle Fortuny, in order to give an hour's private tuition to her eight-year-old granddaughter (his protector, Mr. Bayo, had found him this simple, well-remunerated work), and then return to his apartment in Calle Orellana at about half past nine or shortly thereafter, in time to hear the radio news: although, at first, Lilburn understood almost nothing, he was convinced that this was the best way to learn correct Spanish pronunciation. He then ate a light supper, read a couple of chapters of his Spanish grammar book, hurriedly memorizing vast lists of verbs and nouns, and went to bed punctually at half past eleven. Any reader familiar with the aforementioned Madrid streets and the buildings occupied by the British Institute will have no difficulty in grasping that Lilburn's life could not fail to be anything but methodical and ordered, and that his feet probably took no more than two thousand steps each day. His weekends, however, with the exception of the occasional Saturday when he attended suppers or receptions laid on for visitors to Madrid from British universities (and, on just one occasion, a cocktail party at the embassy), were a mystery to his colleagues and superiors, who supposed—based on the not very revealing circumstance that he never answered the phone on those days—that he must make use of his weekends to go on short trips to nearby towns. It would seem, however, that at least until January or February, young Lilburn spent Saturdays and Sundays closeted in his apartment struggling with the whims and caprices of Spanish conjugations. And one can only assume that he spent his Christmas vacation in the same way.

Derek Lilburn was a man of little imagination, ordinary tastes, and an irrelevant past: the only son of a couple of mediocre, second-tier actors who had achieved a certain degree of popularity (if not prestige) during the early part of the Second World War with an Elizabethan and Jacobean repertoire that included Massinger, Beaumont and Fletcher, and Heywood the Younger, but which scrupulously avoided authors of greater stature like Marlowe, Webster or, indeed, Shakespeare, Lilburn had nonetheless failed to inherit what used to be called "a vocation for the stage"; although one might well question whether his progenitors had ever harbored such a vocation themselves. When the war was over, and the various divas, anxious to resume their positions and hungry for applause, hurried back to the theater with vigor and assiduity, and the slow work of reconstruction as well as the return en masse of the armed forces made London, if not a more anxious city, certainly a more uncomfortable place than when the bombings were rife, the Lilburns, apparently without regret, left the capital and the profession. They settled in Swansea and opened a grocery store, doubtless with the money they had saved during their years devoted to the ignoble and thankless art of acting. All that remained of those eventful times were a few posters advertising *Philaster* and *The Revenger's Tragedy*, and a few facts that have led me, when speaking of his parents, to give more importance to their dramatic incursions—mere anecdote—than to their true status as shopkeepers. Neither books nor erudition filled young Lilburn's childhood, and you can be quite sure that he did not even benefit from the one vestige that might unwittingly have remained of his parents' years spent treading the boards: an emphatic, smug or affected way of speaking even in banal, domestic conversation.

The death of his father, which occurred when young Derek was just eighteen, meant that he could take personal charge of the business, and the death of his mother, a few months later, served as a good excuse to sell the establishment, move to London and pay for his own higher education. Once he had gained his degree, with the deceptive brilliance of the diligent student, he worked as a teacher in state schools for a few years—without, in that brief interval, being assailed by any vocational doubts—until, in 1969, thanks to a superficial and entirely self-interested friendship with one of the teachers at the Polytechnic, he was appointed to the very post he had now rejected in favor of a brief stay abroad—a period which he sensed would somehow be a transitional one.

It is well known to all those familiar with the Institute, whether as teachers, students or merely as regular visitors to the library, that its doors close at nine o'clock sharp (half an hour after the last evening classes end). The person charged with closing up is the porter, to give him his conventional title, even though his duties, and this is more or less the norm in all such coeducational establishments, often depart from those implied by his title and more closely resemble those of a librarian or beadle. This man has to keep an eye on the entrances and exits of anyone not employed by the Institute; attend to any orders, errands or demands issued by teachers; clean the blackboards which, for reasons of carelessness or forgetfulness, have been left, at the end of the day, covered in numbers, illustrious names and notable dates; ensure that no one takes a book from the library without its loan having been duly recorded; and, finally—and leaving aside a few lesser tasks—make quite certain that, at five minutes to nine, the building is empty and, if it is, lock the doors until the following morning. Fabián Jaunedes, the man occupying the busy post of porter when young Derek Lilburn arrived in Madrid, had, for twenty-four years, been carrying out his duties with the perfection of one who has virtually created his own job. And so when, in early March, with some haste and urgency, he was admitted to the hospital for a cataract operation and thus forced to abandon his duties for at least as long as it would take him to recuperate (a recuperation that would necessarily be incomplete or partial and which would, at any rate, take far longer than those running the organization might desire), the internal life of the Institute suffered far worse disruption than one would have thought. The director and Mr. Bayo immediately rejected the idea of taking on a replacement, for, on the one hand, they thought that, at such short notice, it would be hard to find someone with good enough references who would be prepared to commit himself for what little remained of the term, only perhaps to find himself replaced (they doubted the old porter would make such a speedy recovery, but it seemed to them that filling the vacant position for more than five months was tantamount to getting rid of Fabián for good, which would be a gross act of disloyalty to someone who had himself been so loyal and given such good service for so many years). On the other hand, they soon revealed that ability or obscure need to turn a minor sacrifice or compromise into something truly epic—an ability or need so prevalent among the unimaginative and among people of a certain age—when they decided that, in view of this unexpected setback (which they would have described, rather, as an adversity), it would not be unreasonable to call for a minor sacrifice on the part of each and every one of the teachers, who could easily share the absent porter's various duties and demonstrate en passant their selfless devotion to the Institute. The librarian was left in charge of keeping an eye on any strangers who went in and out of the main door, which she could easily see from her usual position; Miss Ferris was to keep the flyers and announcements on the bulletin boards in the entrance hall up to date, although without allowing too many to accumulate; every few hours, Mr. Turol was to inspect the state of the toilets and the boiler; those teachers who finished their classes at half past eight were urged to appoint one of their students to clean the blackboard before leaving; and, lastly, among the members of staff who had not been assigned any specific task, an equitable rota was put in place: someone must remain in the building until nine at night to check that all was in order and to lock the doors. And although this represented a disturbance to Lilburn's rigid routine, he had no alternative but to miss his appointment with Señora Giménez-Klein's granddaughter one evening a week and to collaborate with his superiors and colleagues in the smooth running of the Institute by staying in the library until the usual time of nine o'clock every Friday from March onwards.

It was on the first Friday when he was called upon to perform this new duty that Mr. Bayo revived in his memory—with the same nonchalance that had made an astonished Lilburn wonder if this earnest man with his irreproachable manners was really capable of such an outrageous assertion—that initial warning which, when he'd first arrived, had produced in him a certain feeling of unease.

"Now tonight," Mr. Bayo said to him during break-time, "as I explained to you once before, don't worry about the ghost. I believe I mentioned it briefly when you joined us, but I thought I'd better remind you just in case you'd forgotten, since it's your turn to be on duty and you might be startled by the noises Señor de Santiesteban makes. At a quarter to nine, you'll hear a door burst open, then seven footsteps in one direction and, after a pause, eight footsteps back. The door that opened will then close, more quietly this time. There's no need to be frightened or to take any notice of it. This is something that has been happening since who knows when, certainly for as long as the Institute has had its headquarters in this building. It has nothing whatsoever to do with us and, as you can imagine, we're more than used to it; as, of course, is poor Fabián, who's usually the only person to hear it. Just one thing, given that you will have the keys over the weekend and will, therefore, be the first to arrive on Monday morning to open up, please don't forget to remove his letter of resignation from the bulletin board opposite my office. Be sure to do this as soon as you come in. Although everyone knows of Señor de Santiesteban's existence (we don't hide it from anyone, I can assure you, and no one is troubled or upset by his presence, which is, besides, most discreet), we do nevertheless try not to let it intrude too much on the lives of the students, who, being children, are more sensitive than we are to such inexplicable events. So please do remember to remove the letter. And, of course, simply throw it in the nearest wastepaper basket. Imagine what it would be like if we kept them! By now we'd have a whole roomful of them. When I think about it, it all seems utterly ridiculous! Night after night, at the same hour, the same identical letter, with not a single word or syllable different. That, you'll agree, is what you'd call perseverance."

Young Lilburn responded only with a nod.

But as night fell and he was sitting in the library grading papers until it was time to lock up the building and go home, he heard a door being flung open so violently that it rattled the glass panes, then a few firm, resolute—not to say mutinous—steps, followed by a brief silence that lasted only seconds, then more steps, calmer this time, returning and, finally, the same door (one presumes) gently closing. Lilburn looked at the clock hanging on one wall and saw that it was eight forty-six. Feeling more irritated than surprised or alarmed, he got up and left the library. In the corridor, he stopped and listened, expecting to hear new noises, but there was nothing. Then he scoured the building in search of some laggardly student or joker to whom he would try to demonstrate, more than anything, the pointlessness of his prank, but he found no one. Nine o'clock struck and he decided to leave and give the matter no further thought; however, just as he was about to leave, he remembered another of Mr. Bayo's instructions, possibly the one that had most stuck in his mind: he went up to the second floor to inspect the bulletin board in the corridor, immediately opposite his superior's office. All he saw there, affixed with four thumb tacks, was an already much-read leaflet announcing a series of talks on George Darley and other minor romantic poets that was due to be given by a visiting lecturer from Brasenose College, beginning in April. But there was absolutely nothing remotely resembling a letter of resignation. Feeling calmer and also rather pleased, he set off towards Calle de Orellana and thought no more about the episode until on Monday, around mid-morning, Miss Ferris came up to him after one of his classes and informed him that Mr. Bayo wished to see him in his office.

"Mr. Lilburn," said the old history teacher when he went in, "don't you remember my urging you, before you did anything else this morning, to remove Señor de Santiesteban's resignation letters from the bulletin board outside?"

"Yes, sir, I remember perfectly. But on Friday night, after I'd heard the footsteps you warned me about, I went up to do exactly that, but found no such letters on the board. Should I have looked again this morning?"

Mr. Bayo struck his forehead like someone who has suddenly understood something and replied:

"Of course, it's my fault for not having warned you. Yes, Mr. Lilburn, you need *only* look at the bulletin board in the morning. Not that it matters, this is hardly the first time it's happened. But next Friday, remember: the letter only appears at dawn, even though one would imagine that Señor de Santiesteban would pin it to the noticeboard at a quarter to nine. Yes, I know it's inexplicable, but then so is the very presence of the gentleman himself, is it not? Well, that was all I wanted to say, Mr. Lilburn, but don't worry, the children will have calmed down by this afternoon."

"The children?"

"Yes, it was the juniors who alerted me to the fact that the letters were still there. I heard them talking excitedly in the corridor, went out to see what was going on and found the boys, all very worked up, handing round the three sheets of paper."

Lilburn made an exasperated gesture and said:

"I don't understand a word, Mr. Bayo. I really would be most grateful if you could give me a detailed and coherent account of the facts. What is all this about three letters, for example? What is the story behind this ghost, if he really exists? You keep talking about letters of resignation, but I still don't know what the devil it is that this Señor de Santiesteban fellow resigns from each night. I'm totally bewildered and don't know what to think."

Mr. Bayo gave a faint, melancholy smile and said:

"Nor do I, Mr. Lilburn, and, believe me, after all my years here, I, too, would like to know the details of Señor de Santiesteban's doubtless sad story. But we know absolutely nothing about him. His name tells us nothing, nor, of course, does it appear in any yearbooks, dictionaries or encyclopedias of any kind: he wasn't famous or, rather, he did nothing in his life worthy of mention. Perhaps he was in some way linked to the former owner of the building, the man who had it built around 1930—I can't remember the exact date now: he was an immensely wealthy man, interested in the arts and in politics; he was a kind of patron of left-wing intellectuals during the time of the Second Republic, and he died bankrupt. But we don't know for sure, nor, indeed, do we have any concrete information that allows us to assume any connection. Then again, it could be that his close association with the building stems from his acquaintance, friendship or professional involvement with the architect, who was an equally interesting character: his ideas were quite advanced for the time, but he committed suicide, jumping overboard during an Atlantic crossing when he was still relatively young. Again, there's no way of finding out. All of this is mere supposition, Mr. Lilburn, mere hypothesizing that I don't even dare to formulate in its entirety because there are so few facts."

"It's all very strange, very curious," remarked Lilburn.

"It certainly is," said Mr. Bayo. "And I have to say that a long time ago, when I was only a little older than you are now and had just started work at the Institute, Señor de Santiesteban's mysterious footsteps aroused my curiosity and even robbed me of my sleep for some months; I wouldn't be exaggerating if I said that they came close to becoming an obsession. I neglected my work and devoted myself to making enquiries. I visited the relatives of the former owner and of the architect and asked them about a possible friendship between either of those two men and one Leandro P. de Santiesteban, but they had never heard of him; I consulted old telephone books in search of someone called Pérez de Santiesteban, for example (because I still don't know what the P stands for: perhaps the first part of a double-barrelled last name, perhaps simply Pedro, Patricio, Plácido, I don't know), but I found none; in my overwhelming desire to know the ghost's story, I went to the registry office in the hope that I might find a birth certificate that would at least give me a trail to follow, even if it was a false one: a similar last name so that I could at least focus my investigations on something; but I got no positive results, only problems with various bureaucrats, who took me for a madman, and with the police, because my behavior, in those alarmist times, seemed very suspicious indeed; finally, I went to visit all the Santiestebans in the city, and there are quite a few. But those I spoke with told me there had never been anyone called Leandro in their family, while others refused to even talk to me. In short, it was all in vain and finally I had to abandon my search, with the disagreeable feeling of having wasted my time and made a complete fool of myself. Now, like everyone else who works at the Institute, I simply accept the ghost's undeniable existence and pay him not the slightest heed, because I know there's no point and that taking any interest at all brings only trouble and discontent. And so I'm very sorry, Mr. Lilburn, but I can't answer your questions. I would only advise you to ignore Señor de Santiesteban, like everyone else. Don't worry, he's not dangerous; he simply leaves a resignation letter each night and we remove it the following day."

"That's precisely what I was going to ask you. Doesn't the resignation letter explain something? What is he resigning from? And why, as you said earlier, were there three letters today?"

Mr. Bayo bent towards the wastepaper basket beside him, removed a few crumpled sheets of paper and held them out to Lilburn, saying:

"There were three of them today for the simple reason that today is Monday and, as usual, there was no one in the building over the weekend to take down the letters from Friday, Saturday and Sunday. You should have removed them from the bulletin board first thing this morning, but, as I said, that was my fault, not yours. Here."

Lilburn took the sheets of very ordinary paper and read them carefully. They had been written with a fountain pen, and the words were the same on all three, without the slightest variation:

Dear Friend,

In view of the regrettable events of recent days, the nature of which run counter not only to my habits, but to my principles, I have no alternative, even though I am well aware of the grave difficulties my decision will cause you, of resigning forthwith from my post. And may I say, too, that I strenuously disapprove of and condemn your attitude to the aforementioned events.

Leandro P. de Santiesteban

"As you see," said Mr. Bayo, "the letter reveals nothing, in fact, it only serves to make the whole business even more baffling, given that this building was a private residence and not an office or whatever, that is, not a place occupied by people with posts from which they could resign. We have to be satisfied with merely contemplating the enigma without trying to decipher it."

The months of March and April came and went, and each Friday, young Lilburn, sitting in the library, would listen to Señor de Santiesteban's unvarying footsteps on the floor above. He tried to follow the advice Mr. Bayo had given him and to ignore those mysterious steps, but sometimes, unexpectedly, he would find himself pondering the ghost's personality and history or mechanically counting the number of steps in each direction. In this respect, he had discovered that, as his superior had told him on one occasion, Señor de Santiesteban always took seven steps in one direction and then, after a pause, eight steps back, after which he closed the door.

And it was during the Easter vacation, which he spent in Toledo, that a possible explanation for this occurred to him. He was extremely excited by this tiny discovery—which was, in fact, no more than mere conjecture whose truth he would be unable to verify—and he longed for the moment when he could return to Madrid and tell Mr. Bayo.

And on the first day back after the holidays, instead of staying in the playground during break, exchanging complaints with Miss Ferris and Mr. Bayo about the unsatisfactory behavior of their students, young Lilburn asked Mr. Bayo if they could go somewhere private to talk and, once they were ensconced in the old history teacher's office, he laid his discovery before him.

"In my opinion," he said, slightly nervously, "the reason Señor de Santiesteban takes, first, seven steps and then eight is this: outraged by the events to which he refers in his letter and which prevent him, a man of principle, from remaining in his post, he storms out of the room in which he is sitting and takes seven steps, or should I say strides, over to the bulletin board. He leaves his letter there, and, feeling calmer now that he has done his duty, now that he's broken with the friend who has so disappointed him, and now that his conscience is clear, he returns to his room taking eight steps instead of seven because he is now less angry or agitated, and may even be feeling rather pleased with himself. The proof of this, Mr. Bayo, is the fact that he then closes the door slowly, without the anger evident in the violence with which he flung it open."

"You put the case very well, Mr. Lilburn," replied Mr. Bayo with barely perceptible irony. "And I think you're right. I myself reached the same conclusion many years ago, when I, too, took an interest in the matter. But it got me nowhere imagining that the different number of steps taken in each direction was due to a slight change in Señor de Santiesteban's mood. Here I am, as ignorant as I was on my first day. Listen. The enigma of the Institute's ghost is just that, an enigma. There is no way it can be deciphered."

Mr. Lilburn thought for a moment, somewhat disappointed by Mr. Bayo's cool response. After a few seconds, however, he looked up and asked:

"Wouldn't it be possible to speak to him?"

"Speak to whom? To Señor de Santiesteban? No. Let me explain: on Friday night at a quarter to nine, you hear the door of this office being flung open, as you would on any other evening of the week if you happened to be in the Institute; then you hear footsteps and the door closing again. That's right, isn't it?"

"It is."

"And where are you usually sitting when this happens?"

"In the library."

"Well, if, instead of sitting in the library, you were in this office or, indeed, outside in the corridor, you would hear exactly the same thing, but you would also see that the door does not open. You *hear* it opening and closing, but you can *see* that it neither opens nor closes; it remains in its place, motionless, the glass panes don't even rattle when you hear the door being flung open initially."

"I see. And are you absolutely sure that it's this door and not another door that the ghost opens?"

"Yes. It's definitely that glass-paned door behind you. Believe me, I've checked. When I was sure that this was the case, I spent a few nights here, watching it. As you said before, Señor de Santiesteban storms out of this office, goes over to the bulletin board, pins up his letter of resignation and comes back. The letter, however, doesn't appear at once, but at some point during the night or in the early hours—precisely when I don't know. The only two occasions on which I managed to remain awake, without once nodding off and thus giving Señor de Santiesteban a chance to pin up his letter, I heard the usual footsteps, but the letter never appeared. That must mean that he saw me (saw that I was awake, which is why the letter didn't appear). But he refuses to speak or perhaps cannot speak. After those two nights, when I realized that I, in turn, was being watched by him (or, rather, although I couldn't see him, he was watching my every move), I addressed him on several occasions and in the most diverse tones of voice: one day, I greeted him respectfully, the next mellifluously, the day after that angrily. I even went so far as to insult him, just to see if he would react. But he never responded; nothing worked, and so I did the best thing I could have done: I abandoned my stupid, naive vigils and came to think of Don Leandro P. de Santiesteban just as everyone else here does, as 'the Institute's remarkable ghost.' "

Young Lilburn again thought for a few moments and then said with real concern:

"But, Mr. Bayo, if everything you have told me is true, then Señor de Santiesteban must inhabit this office and might well be listening to us now, isn't that so?"

"Possibly, Mr. Lilburn," responded Mr. Bayo, "possibly."

From that day forth, young Lilburn did not speak to Mr. Bayo or to anyone else about the Institute's ghost. The old teacher assumed, with some relief, that Lilburn had concluded that giving any further thought to the matter was a waste of time and had decided to follow his advice, born of long experience. This was not, however, the case. Young Lilburn, behind his superior's back and in a rather improvised fashion, had decided to find out for himself what it was that drove Señor de Santiesteban to resign from his post every night and, since he was left in charge of the keys of the building over the weekend and could, therefore, come and go as he pleased during those days without having to explain himself to anyone, he had started spending Friday, Saturday and Sunday nights on the sofa in the second-floor corridor, where, even when lying down, he had a clear view of the entire, albeit rather limited stage occupied by the invisible ghost's nocturnal walks, that is, the door of Mr. Bayo's office, the bulletin board opposite and, of course, the space between.

There were three reasons, or, rather, feelings, that drove him to carry out his investigations in secret: suspicion, the lure of the clandestine, and the sheer challenge of the thing. He made good use of Mr. Bayo's generous account of events and of the lessons to be learned from his failure, but, at the same time, he felt that if he was to fulfill his desire to solve the mystery, he had to experience for himself at least some of the setbacks that this same ambition had inflicted on his superior in the past. He also found in those long periods of waiting the pleasure one always gets from experiencing anything that is forbidden or unknown to the rest of humanity. And finally, he savored in advance the moment when his endeavors would be crowned with victory, which consisted not only in securing and forever possessing the longed-for truth, but also in enjoying the inner satisfaction—from which vanity definitely derives the most pleasure—implicit in any triumph over a more important and more knowledgable opponent.

And in the months that followed, the last of the school

year, young Lilburn suffered the same setbacks as the old history teacher had in his youth. He tried without success to speak to Señor de Santiesteban; he waited patiently, again and again, for the letter to appear on the bulletin board, but sooner or later, being obliged as he was to remain for hours with his eyes fixed on one point, sleep almost always overcame him; and on the two or three occasions when he did manage to keep his eyes open until the next morning, the letter did not appear.

Time passed rapidly and he was left with ever fewer opportunities to attain his objective. Dissatisfied with the abominable behavior of his Spanish students and with his work, which had brought him few chances to improve his short-term prospects, he had resolved not to renew his contract for another year and to return to London and to his job at the Polytechnic as soon as the term was over. However, as the end of school activities drew nearer, Lilburn came to regret more and more having made that choice. Now that he had his ticket home, he could not go back on his decision, and he repeatedly berated himself for his precipitate behavior when, in a sudden, irrational rush of confidence, he had thought that success was only a matter of weeks away. He could see the day approaching when he would have to leave, doubtless never to return, and he ceaselessly cursed his excessive optimism and the cold indifference of Señor de Santiesteban, who treated him as haughtily as he had Mr. Bayo, and—even more woundingly—other mere mortals as well. In his madness and while he was listening for the nth time to the sound of the footsteps on the wooden floor, he would try to grab the ghost or shout at him, calling him a vain, cowardly, heartless fraud—in short, heaping him with insults.

However, on just such an occasion, he came up with a

possible remedy for his despair, a solution to his ignorance. A moment before, he had been through one of those stormy episodes provoked by the ghost's disdain for him and, feeling desolate and in the grip of the hysterical rage induced by situations of prolonged impotence, he had lain face down on the sofa in the corridor. It was eight forty-seven. And suddenly, in the midst of his anguish, he seemed to hear the door to Mr. Bayo's office flung open and Señor de Santiesteban again take his invariable fifteen steps before once more closing the door, as he always did. Surprised, he sat up and smoothed his dishevelled hair. He looked at the door and then at the bulletin board. And that was when he realized that he hadn't actually heard anything the second time, but that, like a piece of music on a record one has played and re-played throughout the day, the footsteps (their rhythm and intensity) had lodged in his brain and were being repeated inside him, unwittingly, involuntarily, like an obsessive, particularly complicated passage that one remembers perfectly and yet cannot reproduce. He knew them by heart, and although it was, of course, impossible to imitate them with his voice, he could with his own feet. Buoyed up by new hope and enthusiasm, he left the building. And on that Saturday in June, for the first time in many weekends, he slept in his apartment in Calle de Orellana.

He suddenly felt like an actor who has spent several months performing in the same play with considerable success and who, knowing that the audience will reward his performance with a warm round of applause, is in no hurry to appear on stage to play his part, but rather allows himself the luxury of lingering in the wings and making his entrance a few seconds late so as to create a sense of expectation among the audience and slight alarm among his fellow actors. Lilburn, then, felt so confident of his success that, instead of putting his plan into action right away, he devoted himself—although not without having to struggle against his own pressing feelings of uncertainty—to revelling in the good fortune that destiny, he sensed, was about to bestow on him. He spent only one more typical night at the Institute, on the eve of his encounter with Señor de Santiesteban and of his departure. Indeed, he decided to wait until all the classes and exams were over before carrying out his experiment, and he felt that his last full day would be the most appropriate date to choose, for the following reason: if anything happened to him, anything out of the ordinary, no one would miss him or, in consequence, make any awkward or compromising investigations, given that everyone, including Mr. Bayo, would imagine that he was in London and so would find nothing odd about his absence. And although that night, between eight and half past nine, the students would be putting on their traditional end-of-term theatrical production, which would mean that on that particular Saturday he would be far from alone in the building, he felt that this would, in fact, only work in his favor (on the one hand, no one would trouble him, because at a quarter to nine, parents, teachers, students and cleaning ladies would all be in the auditorium, and, on the other hand, if anyone did surprise him in the act, his presence at that hour in the Institute would be more than justified): all these factors only increased his determination. Just in case, though, he left nothing to chance: he found it easy enough to persuade Mr. Bayo to lend him his office key and to have a copy made; he synchronized his watch with the Institute clock and checked that neither was running slow or fast; and, as I mentioned before, he spent the whole of the previous night rehearsing, until he had an absolutely perfect imitation down.

The day came. Lilburn made his appearance shortly before eight o'clock and was greatly praised for having turned up at the Institute to see the performance even though he was due to fly to London that very night at half past eleven. He took advantage of this circumstance to warn that, precisely because he had a plane to catch, he would, most regrettably, have to leave halfway through the production, adding that he was nevertheless very glad to be able to see at least a good part of it before leaving. Just as the performance was about to begin, he said goodbye to his colleagues and to Mr. Bayo, to whom he said: "You'll be hearing from me."

That year, the students were putting on a shortened version of *Julius Caesar*. Both the acting and the diction were appalling, but Lilburn barely noticed, immersed as he was in his own thoughts. And at twenty-two minutes to nine, at the beginning of the third act, he stood up and, trying not to make too much noise, left the auditorium and walked up to the second floor. He unlocked Mr. Bayo's office door and went in.

There he waited for a few more minutes and then, when it was exactly eight forty-five by his watch and he could hear in the distance the voice of a boy saying "I know not, gentlemen, what you intend, who else must be let blood, who else is rank," young Derek Lilburn flung open the door, making the glass panes rattle, took seven determined steps over to the noticeboard, pinned up a sheet of ordinary paper with one thumb tack, took another eight steps in the opposite direction, went back into the office and closed the door gently behind him.

•

Over the summer, old Fabián Jaunedes lost his sight completely, and Mr. Bayo and the director of the Institute had no option but to hire a new porter. When the new incumbent arrived on September 1st to take up his post, Mr. Bayo told him about Señor de Santiesteban and about the letter of resignation. As he usually did—feeling fearful, moreover, on this occasion that the new arrival might take fright and decide not to accept the post—he tried to play it down and provide as few details as possible. The new porter, who, as well as having impeccable references, had excellent manners and knew his place, merely nodded respectfully and assured Mr. Bayo that he would remember to remove the letter from the bulletin board each morning. The old history teacher breathed a sigh of relief and told himself that acquiring the services of such a man had been a real coup. However, imagine his surprise the next morning, when the new porter came into his office and said:

"I've taken the letter down from the bulletin board, sir, but I just wanted to say that the information you gave me yesterday wasn't quite accurate. Last night, exactly as you warned me I would, I heard the door opening and a few footsteps, but I also clearly heard the voices of two people talking animatedly. This morning, I took down the letter as requested, and I hope you'll forgive me, sir, but purely out of curiosity, I read the letter and I have to say that not only is it not written by just one ghost, as you gave me to understand yesterday, it is signed by two people. See for yourself."

Mr. Bayo took the letter and read it. And while he read, his face assumed an expression similar to that of the teacher who discovers one day that his pupil has outdone him, and—

filled by a strange mixture of envy, pride and fear—can only wonder in confusion whether, in the future, he will find himself humbled or praised by the person who will, from now on, be the one wielding the power.

(1975)

THE LIFE AND DEATH OF MARCELINO ITURRIAGA

November 22nd, 1957, was very overcast. A dense, inert, impenetrable mass of cloud filled the horizon, and a storm was threatening.

The day was of particular significance to me. A year ago exactly, I had left my loved ones, never to return. It was the first anniversary of my death. In the morning, my wife, Esperancita, had brought a bouquet of flowers, which she very carefully placed on top of me. I rather wished she hadn't because the flowers blocked my view, but the twenty-second of each month was her day for bringing me fresh flowers and, on alternate months, the two boys came as well. It was their month to visit, but it being the first anniversary, I imagine Esperancita preferred to come alone. For this same reason, the bunch of carnations was larger than usual and so blocked my view even more. I was able to get a good look at Esperancita though. She was a little plumper than last month and clearly no longer the slender, graceful, agile girl to whom I had once felt so attracted. She moved rather awkwardly and clumsily, and the black mourning clothes she was still wearing really didn't suit her at all. Dressed like that, she reminded me very much of my mother-in-law, for Esperancita's hair was no longer jet black, but was beginning to go white around her forehead and temples. I remembered how she had looked the last time I saw her with my eyes open, and along with that scene, which had taken place a year ago in my apartment in Calle Barquillo, my whole life rose up before me too.

II

I was born in Madrid in 1921, in a small apartment on Calle de Narváez. My father owned the pharmacy downstairs, above which hung a sign saying: ITURRIAGA. PHARMACIST, and just below that in smaller letters: "We Also Sell Candy," which was why my brother and I spent a large part of the day in the store. The rest of the time we were stuck in a dirty old classroom in the local school, where one teacher taught fourteen of us boys all the subjects then on the curriculum. The classes were dull in the extreme, and we either dozed or flicked little balls of paper at each other.

My mother was a plump, placid woman, who always helped my brother and me whenever we had a problem or when my father, after a day of poor sales, vented his frustration on us.

My father was a most irascible man, especially when he was in a bad mood, and I always thought he would have been far better suited to being a butcher or something, rather than a pharmacist.

I stayed at that school in Calle de Narváez until I was fifteen, and then the Civil War broke out, but that passed me by as just another of life's events. It brought neither me nor my family any great losses. My brother fought at the front, but survived unscathed and returned home full of a patriotism and a pride in the right-wing Nationalist victory that I never shared. Then I began a degree in economics, which took me eight years to complete, much to the displeasure of my father, who disapproved of all those delays and repeated courses. Despite everything, though, I think my time as a student was the happiest and liveliest of my brief life. I had fun, studied very little and met Esperancita. She was rather shy with boys, but was nonetheless affectionate and obliging. We used to go to the cinema or the circus or for a walk, and ended up spending nearly every afternoon or evening together. Two years after finishing my degree, I asked Esperancita to marry me. She said "Yes," and two years later, my first son, Miguel, was born, and two years after that, Gregorito, a name I never liked, but which I had to accept at the insistence of my mother-in-law, who was called Gregoria. Besides, I always thought the name "Gregorito Iturriaga Aguirre" was too long and had too many *r*s.

Now that I think about it, I don't believe I married Esperancita for love, but because I thought she would be a real help to me in my work at the bank. As it turned out, however, she wasn't much help at all, because she took bringing up the children far too seriously and spent all day with them. I wasn't particularly happy with her, but I wouldn't say I was particularly unhappy either.

Living with us were my mother-in-law and my father, who couldn't stand the sight of each other, but since they had to, and given that the apartment was fairly small, they spent all day fighting and arguing over stupid things about which they couldn't—or, rather, shouldn't—have argued, because they knew almost nothing about them. This, along with Esperancita shouting at Manuela the maid and the children crying, made home unbearable, and the bank seemed to me a paradise. With seven mouths to feed, I was always glad to work overtime, but I did so largely because it gave me more quiet time to myself.

My mother died four years after the war ended, and she was, I believe, the only person I was ever really fond of. I was much more upset by her death than by that of my father, for whom I had never felt any real filial affection.

III

My death came as pretty much of a shock to everyone. In August 1956, I began to experience intense stabbing pains in my chest. Alarmed, I consulted my brother, who was a doctor.

He reassured me, saying that it was probably just the aftereffects of a bad cold or a sore throat.

He wrote me out a prescription for some pills, and the pain went away until November 16th, when it attacked with even more fury than in August. I started taking the pills again, but this time they brought me no relief, and the 21st found me in bed with a high temperature, lung cancer and no hope of surviving.

That was an extremely distressing day. The pain was terrible and no one could do anything to relieve it. I could vaguely make out Esperancita, who was kneeling by my bed, weeping, while my mother-in-law, Doña Gregoria, patted her fondly and consolingly on the back. The children barely moved at all, unable to understand what was going on. My brother and his wife were sitting down as if waiting for me to die so that they could make their exit from that tedious, melodramatic scene. My boss and some of my colleagues were standing in the doorway, watching me pityingly, and whenever they saw that I was looking at them, they would give very forced friendly smiles. At six o'clock on the evening of the 22nd, when the fever intensified, I tried to get out of bed, but fell back against the pillow, dead. At the moment of death, I felt all my pain and suffering vanish and I wanted to tell my family and friends that I was no longer in pain, that I was alive and well, but I couldn't. I couldn't speak or move or open my eyes, even though I could see and hear everything going on around me. My mother-in-law said:

"He's dead."

"May he rest in peace," chorused the others.

I saw how my brother and his wife immediately withdrew, once they had told Esperancita that they would take care of the funeral, due to take place the following day. Gradually, everyone else went too, and I was left alone. I didn't know what to do. I could think, see and hear, therefore I existed, therefore I was alive, and the next day they were going to bury me. I tried desperately to move, but couldn't. Then I realized that I was dead, that beyond death there was nothing, and all that remained for me was to lie in my grave forever, not breathing, but alive; without eyes, but able to see; without ears, but able to hear.

The next day, they put me in a black coffin and then in the hearse that took me to the cemetery. Not many people turned up. After the brief service, everyone left and I was alone. At first, I didn't like it here at all, but I'm used to it now, and I enjoy the silence. I see Esperancita once a month, and the boys every other month, and that's all: this is my life and my death, where there is nothing.

(1968)

ISAAC'S JOURNEY

He devoted his whole life to trying to resolve an enigma.

When his best friend's father, Isaac Custardoy by name, was still a young man, a threat, a curse or a malediction was put on him. He lived in Havana and was a landowner and a soldier; he would boast about his career and his reputation as a ladies' man and had no plans to marry, at least not until he was fifty or so. When he was out riding one morning, he passed a mulatto beggar, whose request for alms he refused. Just as he was about to ride off and had dug in his spurs, the beggar grabbed the reins of his horse and said: "You and your eldest son and the eldest son of your eldest son will all die when you are far from your own country; you will never reach fifty and you will receive no burial." His friend's father paid little heed; when he returned home from his ride, he told the story over lunch and promptly forgot all about it. This happened in 1873, when his friend's father was only twenty-five.

In 1898, by which time he, the best friend's father, was a lieutenant colonel and married with seven children, it was clear that Commodore Schley was sure to win and that Cuba was about to fall to a foreign power, and he could not bear the thought of seeing anything other than a Spanish flag flying over the port of Havana. He hurriedly sold off all his possessions, hardened himself to the idea of leaving his native land for good and, despite never having left the island before and despite suffering from Ménière's disease, he embarked for Spain along with all his family. After only a week on board ship, a particularly virulent attack of said disease ended his life: he was leaning on the rail up on deck, thinking and wondering (even allowing himself a frisson of excitement): what would it be like, that country whose name he knew so well? Suddenly, doubtless after being assailed by terrible noises and then by silence—to judge by his brief frantic gestures, first, of pain and, then, of stupefaction—he dropped dead. A cannonball was attached to his corpse and he was thrown overboard. He was about to turn fifty.

In Spain, the eldest son, also called Isaac Custardoy, continued the military career he had begun in Cuba under the auspices of his father. Possessed of a genuine vocation and great determination, he rose very swiftly to the rank of colonel and became aide-de-camp to General Fernández Silvestre. He lived in Madrid and, having always felt responsible for his younger siblings, watched over them and rarely left the city. In 1921, however, he had no option but to accompany his friend and commanding officer to Morocco. In the midst of the disastrous battle of Annual, when the Spanish troops had been scattered and defeated by the berbers of Abd-el-Krim, the General, Custardoy, and the general's son, victims of the prevailing mayhem, mass panic and confusion, found themselves helpless and cut off from the rest of the main group; they did, however, have a truck at their disposal. Silvestre refused to leave the field and Custardoy refused to leave his commanding officer; between them, though, they persuaded the general's son to drive to safety in the truck. The two soldiers were left to face the rout alone and their bodies were never found. Of Custardoy they retrieved only his field glasses and his leather belt. The two men had presumably been impaled. Isaac Custardoy was forty-five years of age. He left only a wife.

Isaac Custardoy's best friend spent his whole life trying to resolve that enigma: why had the mulatto beggar's prediction been so absolutely right on two counts, but not on the third? The eldest son had no eldest son. The idea of an illegitimate heir was simply too banal. If none of the curse had been fulfilled, or if all of it had, then he would have been able to rest easy. Instead, he devoted his whole life to resolving the enigma.

When he was old and bored with doing nothing, he used to enjoy reading the Bible. And one day, re-reading it for the nth time, he paused over the words: *And Abraham was fourscore and six years old when Hagar bare Ishmael to Abraham.* Further on, he paused again: *And Abraham was a hundred years old when his son Isaac was born unto him.* Yahweh had announced the birth of Isaac long before Ishmael, the son of Hagar, had been born—indeed, he was already thirteen when Sarah gave birth. This gave him cause to reflect: "Where was Isaac all that time, from the moment when his birth was prophesied to the moment when he was born, from the moment when his existence was predicted to the actual moment of conception?" Well, he must have been somewhere, because Yahweh knew about him, as did Abraham and Sarah. This led him still further on, to his problem; it led him to think: "The birth of Isaac Custardoy's grandson had been prophesied too, but he was never born, neither born nor engendered. But the mulatto beggar and Custardoy himself had known about him since 1873. Where had he been since then? He must have been somewhere."

He continued to ponder this and devoted what remained of his life to resolving the enigma. And when he was close to death, he wrote his thoughts down on a piece of paper: "I sense that I am about to die, to set off on my final journey. What will become of me? Where will I go? Will I go anywhere? I can sense the approach of death because I have lived and was engendered, because I'm still alive; death, therefore, is not perfect or all-embracing, it cannot prevent something other than itself from existing; it has to put up with the fact that something waits for it and thinks about it. Someone who has not been born or, even more so, someone who has not even been engendered or conceived is the one thing that belongs to death entirely. The person who has not been conceived dies most. He or she has traveled unceasingly along that most tortuous and labyrinthine of paths: the path of contingency. He or she is the only one who will have neither homeland nor grave. That person is Isaac Custardoy. I, on the other hand, I am not."

(1978)

WHAT THE BUTLER SAID

For Domitilla Cavalletti

On a recent brief stay in New York, one of the two things that Europeans most dread happening to them happened: I was trapped for half an hour in an elevator between the twenty-fifth and twenty-sixth floors of a skyscraper. I don't, however, want to talk about the fear I felt nor the more than justified claustrophobia that made me shout out (yes, I admit it) every few minutes, but about the man who was riding with me when the elevator stopped and with whom I shared that half hour of confidences and terror. He was immaculately dressed and extremely circumspect (in that difficult situation, he only shouted once and stopped when he realized that we had been heard and located). He looked exactly like the butlers you see in movies and, as it turned out, he was a butler in real life. In exchange for a little incoherent, disparate information about my country, he gave me the following account of his life while we waited in that large vertical coffin: he was working for a wealthy young couple comprising the president of one of the largest and most famous American cosmetic companies and his recently acquired European wife. They lived in a five-story mansion; they traveled around the city in an eight-door limousine with smoked-glass windows (like the one belonging to the late President Kennedy, he added), and he, the butler, was one of their four servants (all of them white, he said). The butler's hobby was black magic, and he had already managed to obtain a lock of his young mistress's hair, having cut it off while she was taking a nap in an armchair one very hot, very sleepy afternoon. He told me all this quite calmly, and despite my own panic, I managed to listen to him relatively calmly. I asked him why he had so cruelly cut off that lock of hair. Had she perhaps mistreated him?

"'Not yet,' he replied, 'but sooner or later she will. It's a precautionary measure. Besides, if something does happen, how else could I exact my revenge? How can a man avenge himself these days? Besides, the practice of black magic is very fashionable in America. Isn't it in Europe?' I told him that, with the possible exception of Turin, it was not and asked if he couldn't use his black magic to get us out of that elevator. 'The kind of magic I practice can only be used for acts of revenge. Who do you want us to take our revenge on, the elevator company, the architect, Mayor Koch? We might succeed, but that wouldn't get us out of here. Besides, it won't be long now.' It wasn't long, in fact, and once the elevator was moving again and we had reached the ground floor, the

butler wished me a pleasant stay in his city and vanished as if our half hour together had never existed."

Thus began an article which, under the heading "Vengeance and the Butler," I published in the Spanish newspaper El País *on Monday, December 21st, 1987. Then the article lost sight of the butler and turned its attentions to the subject of revenge. It was not, therefore, the right place in which to transcribe in detail everything that my traveling companion had told me, indeed, on that occasion, I altered one fact completely and said nothing about the rest. Perhaps I did this because the queen of the cosmetics company was also Spanish. She might, I thought, be a reader of* El País, *or perhaps, if I stuck too closely to the facts, some acquaintance of hers in Spain might recognize her and pass on the article. I confess that I was guided more by the desire not to get the butler into trouble than by any desire to alert the queen to some hypothetical danger. This is perhaps the moment though, now that my gratitude towards the former has somewhat faded and the chances of the latter ever reading this story are infinitely fewer. Not that I have any other means of alerting her, not at least discreetly. While she may read newspapers, I doubt very much that she reads books, certainly not stories written by a compatriot. But that won't be my fault: the books we don't read are full of warnings; we will either never read them or they will arrive too late. Anyway, my conscience will be clearer if I give her the possibility, however remote, of taking precautions, but without my feeling that I have also betrayed the butler who so kindly reassured me and helped make that wait in the elevator more bearable. The one fact I had changed in my article was that the marriage was not so very recent and so the butler was not, as I had him say, awaiting any possible future affronts from his mistress: he was in fact, according to him, already a constant victim of such affronts.*

What follows are his words, insofar as I can now remember and set them down, although not in any very orderly fashion, since I no longer feel able to reproduce that conversation accurately, and can only recall a few of the things he said. JM

The butler said:

"I don't know if all Spanish women are the same, but the one example I've known is truly horrible. She's vain, rather dim, and very rude and cruel, and I hope you'll forgive me speaking like this about a woman from your country."

"That's fine, feel free, say anything you like," I replied generously, although without paying much attention.

The butler said:

"I realize that what I'll say will have little authority or value, and could simply be interpreted as my getting something off my chest. I wish the world was made in such a way that there could be some direct confrontation between us—between my accusations and hers, or between my accusations and her defense—without grave consequences for me, by which I mean dismissal. There aren't that many families who can take on a butler, not even in New York—there aren't a lot of jobs out there—very few people can afford one servant, let alone four, as my employers can. Things were pretty much perfect until she arrived, for my boss is very pleasant and hardly ever at home, and he was single when I started working for him five years ago. Well, he was divorced actually, and that's my one hope really, that he'll end up divorcing her too, sooner or later. But it might be later, and it's best to be prepared. I've finished my course in black magic now. Most of it was by correspondence initially, and then I had a few practical lessons. I have my diploma. Not that I've done much with it. We get together occasionally to kill a chicken, very unpleasant, as you can imagine—you get covered in feathers, the bird puts up quite a fight, you know, but we have to sacrifice something now and then, because, if we didn't, our organization would lose all credibility."

I remember that this last comment worried me briefly and made me listen much more closely, and that's why, hoping my fear might be dissipated by another greater fear, I banged on the elevator door again, pressing the alarm button and the buttons for all the other floors and shouting out several times: "Hey! Listen! We're still trapped in here! We're still in here!"

The butler said:

"Take it easy, nothing's going to happen to us. It's a big elevator, there's plenty of air, and they know we're here. People may be pretty callous these days, but they're not likely to forget two people trapped in an elevator, and besides, they need to get it working again. Now, my mistress, your compatriot, she really is callous, she mistreats everyone, or, worse, ignores them. She has the ability, which is perhaps more common in Europe than in the United States, to talk to us as if we weren't there, without looking at us, without noticing us, she speaks to us without actually addressing us, exactly as if she were talking about us to a friend. A little while ago, an Italian girlfriend of hers came to stay, and although they were talking in one of their languages, neither of which I understand, I could tell that a lot of their conversations were about us, and about me in particular, because I've been there the longest. so I suppose in a way I'm in charge of the other servants. She can make a remark about me in my presence without giving the slightest hint that she's talking about me, but her friend, lacking that talent, couldn't help shooting me the occasional furtive glance with her green eyes as they chatted away in their Latin languages, whichever one it was. On the other hand, during the weeks that her friend was in the house, she did, at least, have other things to think about and took less notice of me. Let me explain, she's been here for three years now, but she still speaks English really badly, with a very strong accent, so much so that sometimes I find it hard to understand her, and this irritates her of course, because she thinks I do it on purpose to offend her, which is partly true, but I can assure you that most of the time it's simply because I don't always make the necessary effort to understand her, that effort of comprehension and listening, or sometimes guessing. The truth is that after three years, even a city like New York can become wearisome and tedious if you have nothing to do. My boss goes to work every morning and doesn't get back until late, until the Spanish time for supper, which she has imposed on him. You may not realize it, but cosmetics are a complicated business: like pharmaceuticals, you constantly have to research and perfect them, you can't just settle for a fixed range of products. According to him, there are incredible advances made every year, every month, and you have to keep up to date, just like with drugs. Anyway, he works for twelve hours or more, and is only home at night and on the weekends, and that's about it. Naturally, she gets pretty bored, because she's bought just about everything she can buy for the house, although she still keeps an eye out for any novelties: any new product or gadget or invention, any new fashion, any new Broadway show or exhibition or movie, she immediately gloms onto them, more quickly than even a city like this can cope with."

By this point, I was sitting on the elevator floor. He, on the other hand, immaculate and circumspect, remained standing, still in coat and gloves, one hand resting on the wall and one foot elegantly crossed over the other. His shoes were unnaturally shiny.

The butler said:

"So generally speaking, she's at home, with nothing to do, apart from watching television and making long-distance calls to her friends in Spain, inviting them to visit, not that they often do, which is hardly surprising. When she can't talk any more, when she's tired from so much talking and her eyes hurt from watching so much TV, then the only thing she can think of is to fixate on me, because I'm always home, or almost always, I'm the one who knows where everything is or where to find things if we have to send out for something. She fixates on me, you see, and there's nothing worse than being someone's sole source of distraction. Sometimes she betrays herself, or, rather, betrays her usual disdainful self: without realizing it, she'll find that for some minutes she hasn't been giving me orders or asking me pointless questions, but has actually been talking to me—imagine that, conversing."

I remember that, at this point, I got up and pounded on the door again with the flat of my hand. I was about to shout out again too, but decided to follow the example of the butler, who spoke very calmly, as if we were, in fact, outside the elevator, waiting for it to arrive. I remained standing, like him, and asked:

"What do you talk about?"

The butler said:

"Oh, she makes some remark about something she's read in a magazine or about some contest she's seen on TV. There's one particular show that's on every evening at half past seven, just before my boss gets home, *Family Feud*, she's crazy about it and everything has to stop at half past seven so that she can give it her full attention. She turns out the lights, leaves the phone off the hook, and during the half hour that *Family Feud* lasts, we could do absolutely anything, even set the house on fire, and she wouldn't notice; we could go into her bedroom, where she watches TV, and burn the bed, and she wouldn't notice. During that time, the only thing that exists is the TV screen. I've only seen that capacity for total concentration in children, but then she is rather like a child. While she's watching *Family Feud*, I could commit murder, I could slit the throat of one of our chickens behind her back and scatter its blood and feathers over her sheets, and she wouldn't notice. When the half hour was up, she'd get to her feet, look around her and scream: 'Where has all this blood and feathers come from? What's happened?' But she wouldn't have noticed me slitting the chicken's throat. We could steal paintings, furniture, jewelry, we could bring our friends over and have an orgy on her bed while she's watching *Family Feud*. We don't, of course, because it's also our boss's bed, and we like and respect him. But I'm not exaggerating when I say that we could even rape her while she's watching *Family Feud*, and she wouldn't notice. Before I realized this, I always had to find an opportune moment, as I explained, to snip off a lock of her hair or steal an item of clothing, underwear or whatever, a handkerchief or some stockings. But now, if I wanted to steal some personal possession of hers, I'd just wait until half past seven from Monday to Friday and take what I wanted while she watched her show. I'll tell you something, just so you can see that I'm *not* exaggerating. I conducted an experiment once, which is why I say that we could rape her and she wouldn't notice. On one occasion, I went up behind her while she was watching *Family Feud.* She sits very close to the screen, very upright on a kind of low stool, probably thinking that the discomfort will help her to concentrate. One evening, I approached her from behind and touched her shoulder with my gloved hand, as if I wanted to get her attention. She insists that I always wear gloves, you see, I only have to put on full livery when there are guests for supper, but she likes me to wear my white silk gloves all the time, in the belief that a butler should be constantly running his finger over every surface, over the furniture and along the banisters, to check for dust, because if there is any dust, the gloves will pick it up immediately. Anyway, I always wear them, but they're so fine that it's almost like not wearing gloves at all. So, I touched her shoulder with my sensitive fingers, and when she took no notice, I left my hand there for a few seconds and gradually increased the pressure. So far, nothing very out of the ordinary. She didn't turn round, didn't move, nothing. Then I moved my hand—I was still standing up—stroking rather than squeezing her shoulders and collarbone, and she remained utterly impassive. I began to wonder if perhaps she was inviting me to go further, and I have to admit that I'm still not sure; but I don't think so, I still believe she was just so absorbed in watching *Family Feud* that she didn't notice anything. And so I slid my gloved hand towards her cleavage, she always wears very low-cut tops, too low-cut for my taste, but my boss, on the other hand, likes it, I've heard him say so. I touched her bra, which was a bit rough to the touch to be honest, and it was that, rather than any desire on my part, that persuaded me to avoid the bra or, shall we say, arrange things so that its fabric only rubbed against the back of my hand, which is less sensitive than the palm, even though I was wearing my gloves. I'm not much for the ladies, I barely have anything to do with them, but skin is skin, flesh is flesh. And so for several long minutes I stroked one breast and then the other, left and right, breast and nipple, it was very pleasant, and she didn't move or say anything, didn't even change position while she was watching her show. I think I could have carried on if *Family Feud* lasted longer, but then I saw that the host was about to say goodnight and I withdrew my hand. I was able to tiptoe backwards out of the room before she emerged from her trance. My boss got home that night at eight o'clock on the dot—and the theme tune was still playing on the TV."

"Are you sure they're going to get us out of here? They're taking forever," I said as my only response, and again shouted out and beat the metal door. "Hey! Come on!"

The butler said:

"I've told you, they won't be much longer. Each minute may seem like an hour to us, but in reality a minute only ever lasts a minute. We haven't been in here for as long as you think, just take it easy."

I again slid down to the floor and stayed there, leaning my back against the wall (I had taken off my overcoat and draped it over my arm).

"Did you ever touch her again?" I asked.

The butler said:

"No. That was before the little girl died, and she disgusts me so much now that I wouldn't even stroke her finger. A year ago, she became pregnant. My boss had no children from his previous marriage, so this would be his first child. You can imagine what the pregnancy was like, a real nightmare as far as I was concerned: it meant double the work and double the attention that she always demands of me—she was constantly summoning me to ask the most stupid, useless things. I really considered quitting then, but, as I say, there's not much work around. When she gave birth, I was pleased, not just for my boss, but because the child would become her main source of distraction, relieving me of that role. The little girl, however, was born with a serious defect. She would only survive a matter of months, but if you don't mind, I'd rather not go into detail. As I say, it was clear from the start that the child was doomed, that she wouldn't live for more than a few months, three, four, six, or, at the most, a year. Now I realize how hard that is, I understand how, knowing this, a mother might not want to grow too attached to her child, but for as long as the baby lives, she deserves to be cared for and loved, don't you think? After all, the only thing that marked the baby out from the rest of us was that she had a known expiration date, because we all expire at some point, don't we? When the mother found out what was going to happen, she wanted nothing to do with her. She more or less handed the child over to us, the servants, she even brought in a woman to feed her and change her diapers, so there were five of us in the house during those months, but now there's just the four of us again. My boss didn't get very involved either, but then that's different, he works such long hours he wouldn't have had the time anyway, even if the child had been healthy. She, as usual, was mostly at home, more than she would have liked, and yet she never went into the baby's room, not even with her husband to say good night to her, well, hardly ever. He used to, though, on his own, before retiring to bed. I would go with him and stand on the threshold, my white hand holding the door open so as to let in a little light from the corridor; he didn't dare turn on the light in the room, probably so as not to wake her, but also, I think, so that he would only just see her in the half-dark. But at least he saw her. He would go and stand by the crib, although not too close, a few feet away, and from there he would watch her and listen to her breathing, just for a while, a minute or less, enough to say good night. When he left, I would stand to one side, I would push open the door for him with my gloved hand and watch him walk to his bedroom, where she would be waiting. I, on the other hand, did go into the baby's room and I'd sometimes stay there for a long time. I'd talk to her. I don't have any children of my own, but it just seemed natural to talk to her, even if she couldn't understand and even without the excuse that she needed to grow accustomed to the human voice. The sad thing is that she didn't need to grow accustomed to anything, she had no future, nothing awaited her, she had no reason to get used to anything, it was a waste of time. In the house, no one talked about her or mentioned her, as if she had already ceased to exist before she died—that's the unfortunate thing about knowing the future. Even we, the servants I mean, didn't talk about her, but most of us would go up and visit her, on our own, as if we were visiting a shrine. My black magic, of course, couldn't cure her—as I said it can only be used for revenge. She, the mother, got on with her life, phoning Madrid or Seville, which is where she's from, talking to her friend when she was here, going out shopping and to the theater, or watching television and *Family Feud* from Monday to Friday, at half past seven. After that time when I touched her, without her realizing, I had, how can I put it, begun to feel almost fond of her. Contact does create affection, a little, no matter how minimal that contact is, don't you think?"

The butler paused long enough for his last comment not to appear rhetorical, and I stood up and said:

"Yes, that's why you have to be careful who you touch."

The butler said:

"Exactly, you might not think much of someone or even think very badly of them, then suddenly, one day, by chance, on impulse, out of weakness, loneliness, fear or drunkenness, one day, you find yourself caressing the person you'd thought so little of. That doesn't mean you change your mind about them, but you do grow fond of someone you've caressed or who has allowed themselves to be caressed. And I had acquired a little of that elementary affection for her, after caressing her breasts with my white gloves while she was watching *Family Feud*—that was at the beginning of her pregnancy, during which, because of that incipient affection, I was more patient than usual and brought her whatever she wanted without complaint. Afterwards, I lost that affection, well, after the baby was born. But what made me lose it once and for all—what caused me to feel only disgust for her—was the death of the child, who survived for even less time than expected, two and a half months, not even three. My boss was away, he still is, I told him about the death yesterday by phone, he didn't say much, just: "Oh, so it's happened." Then he asked me to take care of everything, of the cremation or burial, leaving it to me to choose, perhaps because he realized that, in the end,

I was the person closest to the child. I was the one who picked her up from her crib and called the doctor, I was the one who, this morning, removed her sheets and her little pillow—I don't know if you realize this, but they make tiny sheets for newborn babies, and tiny pillows too. This morning, I told her, the mother, that I was going to bring the child here, to the thirty-second floor, to have her cremated: they offer a very high-quality service, one of the best in New York; they really know their business; they occupy a whole floor. And what do you think she said? 'I don't want to know anything about it.' 'I thought you would want to come with me, to accompany her on her last journey,' I said. And what do you think she said? She told me: 'Don't be so stupid.' Then, since I would be in this part of town, she asked me to get some tickets to the opera for some friends who are coming over in a few weeks' time. She, of course, has a season ticket. She has a future, you see, unlike the baby. So I came on my own with the baby inside her little coffin, as white as my white silk gloves. I could have carried it in my own hands, white on white, my gloves on the coffin. I didn't need to, though. The very efficient company on the thirty-second floor had thought of everything, and they came for us this morning in a hearse and brought us here. She, the mother, leaned over the banister, on the fourth floor, just as I was about to leave with the child and the coffin, because I was already going out the door with my coat and my gloves on. And do you know what her final words were? She shouted down at me in that strong Spanish accent of hers: 'Make sure they have lots of carnations, lots of carnations, and orange blossom!' That was the only instruction she gave. Now my hands are empty, I've just come from the cremation." The butler glanced at his watch for the first time since we'd been stuck in the elevator and added: "We've been here nearly half an hour."

Orange blossom, he had said: the flowers that brides in Andalusia wear, I thought. But just then the elevator began to move again and, when we reached the ground floor, the butler wished me a pleasant stay in his city and vanished, as if the half hour that had brought us together had never existed. He was wearing black leather gloves, which he kept on all the time.

(1990)